The Last Time I Saw Her

The Gossamer and Pitch Trilogy: Book Three

Jae Mazer

A HellBound Books® LLC Publication

SIGN UP FOR THE HELLBOUND BOOKS NEWSLETTER:

www.hellboundbooks.com

Printed in the United States of America

Also by Jae Mazer

Novels

- Landing in Eden
- Delivery
- Pal Tailor
- Gahl's Door
- Chrysalis and Clan
- Notch (written as J.M. Adler)
- Crone: A Witch's Tale
- Beautiful Beasts: A Collection of Visceral Horror
- Ripples of Silence (co-authored with Gerry Mazer)
- Tales from the Den (co-authored with Jessica Raney)
- The Sisters Three
- Tales from Ramnon
- Mister Picket Blackmaw
- Sometimes We Don't Escape
- Salt of my Blood
- Mother Mare

Inclusion in Magazines and Anthologies:

- *The Wish* in Sicklit Magazine
- *Flight of the Crow* in Eclectically Heroic by Inklings Publishing
- *The Waif and the Witch* in Hair-Raising Tales of Villainous Confessions by Madgirl Publishing
- *Hurt* in Hair-Raising Tales of Villainous Confessions by Madgirl Publishing
- *The Ballad of Big Sammy Purdue* In Monster Party
- *Death Served* in Books of Horror Volume I
- *Of Your Own Creation* in Books of Horror Volume 2

- *Mozart in the Flames* in Books of Horror Volume 3, Part One
- *Blubber Murray* in Twisted Legends by From the Ashes Press
- *That's a Peculiar Stain on the Carpet ...* In Roadkill Texas Volume 8
- *I Didn't Hate This Goodbye* in Dead Heat: An Anthology of Summer Horror by From the Ashes Press
- *Behold, Death Arrives, A Duet of Ash and Fang* in These Lingering Shadows by Last Waltz Publishing.
- *Aisle Four* in Trapped: A Dark Dozen Anthology from Uncomfortably Dark Publishing
- *The Rise and Fall of the Corn Kings of Appalachia* in Harvested: An Anthology of Reaping What You Sow by From the Ashes Press
- *That's a Mighty Fine Head of Hair You've Got There* in Head Blown Too by Merrill David and Texas Authorcon
- *To Never Know* In Lucky Number 13 by Limitless Ink Press
- *Please* In Deviants and Decadence by Stitched Smile publishing LLC

Audioplays/Dramatizations:

Down with the Ship: Episode on July 27th, 2021 of Hearing the Haunted: A Sirenicide Production

Straight on Through: Episode on January 25th, 2021 in Hearing the Haunted: A Sirenicide Production

The Last Time I Saw Her

Chapter One

The last time I saw her, I was dead. I was in a grave, looking up at the sky, stars like speckled paint across the never-ending indigo. There was an earthworm crawling through my sinuses. I realized, after noticing it slithering through my facial cavities, that my mouth was full of wet dirt. Packed full, puffing my cheeks out like a squirrel's. Then the stars disappeared, eclipsed by a looming shape.

Her face and body were dark, a silhouette against the night sky, but her eyes were glowing. I recognized her eyes, though they were eyes she'd never had. One blue, one dark hazel, twinkling with stars of their own. Her hair on one side was an explosion of curls, the other a shorn pixie cut. She reached for me, down into the grave, and laced her fingers through mine. Her hands were cold and wet, then warm and soft. Pain and pleasure radiated from her touch, my vagina tearing all the way to my anus, my body pulsating with endorphins, the rapid growth of my bones and stretching of my skin until the grave was too small, and I was too big, and I had to curl to fit as dirt rained down upon me.

"Ah, hhiiiit," I tried to curse, but my words couldn't find their way through the clumps of soil packed in my maw.

It happened again. I couldn't believe it kept happening. My body was naked and exposed, gleaming with sweat, my nipples dark and erect, sweat slick between my thighs and beneath my breasts and arms. It was a humid autumn made worse by the lush woods surrounding the cemetery hidden beyond Eden's Edge. Those woods held moisture like they held spirits.

I clawed and scrambled my way out of the grave. Once I was on the right side of the grass, I rolled over on my back and stared at the moon.

Four in the morning.

I knew the sky like my own flesh. One of the perks of being half witch.

What the fuck am I doing?

I had dug quite the hole. Pert near a meter of dirt was piled up beside the grave, and my arms ached from what I could only imagine was the labour of heaving soil for hours. And this was not the first occurrence of a middle-of-the-night escapade. I had woken up more than once in the past four weeks in the same situation—naked and in an open grave. And the times I didn't regain consciousness out in that cemetery behind Eden's Edge, I woke up in my bed with my feet and hands caked in dry mud.

Thankfully I had the most patient, understanding wife in all of existence. She tolerated all my comings and goings, which typically involved some variation of witchcraft or the occult, both of which generated a high degree of mess and chaos. *I* was mess and chaos, and Liza loved me, regardless. Dirt on the floor and in the bed clothes was nothing compared to some of the stuff I'd dragged home in our decades together.

But it was getting worse. It happened once six months ago, then again two months later. Now it was happening twice a week, this self burial in my birthday suit.

I cupped my hands over my face and blew my nose. Globs of snot thick with dirt came out, along with a single earthworm. There were more in there, wriggling and forcing themselves through my narrow tunnels. In fact, they were everywhere—in my veins, my vagina, behind my eyeballs. But it was no mind. I was the dirt, and the dirt was me. I rocked back and landed on my buttocks, lowered myself to a laying position, and spread like a starfish. I bore down, squeezing the worms, guiding them out of my veins, my eye sockets, my anus and urethra.

With my passengers fully expelled, I stood and brushed the muck from my flesh—a futile attempt, given that I was coated from head to toe. My hair was tangled with detritus accumulated from rolling around the forest floor. It would need a wash and a brush at best, scissors at worst. I scratched at a particularly dirty spot on my abdomen, but it wouldn't budge. It was almost like the dirt was beneath my skin, branching out in fat, muddy veins. I examined myself. There were a few more spots like that, one on the top of my foot and a smaller glob on my wrist.

I needed a long, violent shower.

"Where are my clothes?" I said, punctuating the question with a dirt encrusted sigh.

"Gahhhh."

Old Man Merle was a crooked sentry posted at the edge of the cemetery, skeletal finger pointing at the lychgate, which looked more like a mess of trees and bushes with the thick overgrowth obscuring every centimeter of its surface. My clothes were there, neatly folded and placed beneath the arches.

"Thanks, Merle," I said.

"Gahhhh," he answered.

I grabbed my clothes but didn't bother donning them. I was too filthy, and I'd been wearing leggings and a sports bra—both impossible to get on whilst damp. Besides, it would be a bitch to launder them coated in the thick sap and muck of the autumn woods.

"Gahhhh," Merle said again, this time emphatically.

His skeletal finger was pointed at the lychgate. I checked the clothes in my arms.

"I got everything, buddy," I said.

"Gahhhh!" he said.

He stabbed the air with his finger, still pointing at the lychgate.

"What is it—"

The blank tendrils of dirt on my skin. They were also on the lychgate. And the ground, though it was hard to tell in the dark. Could have been dirt, roots, worms. But it sure looked like something foreign.

"It's late," I said, turning from the mystery. "And dark. This can wait until the morning."

I started my journey back through the woods with Old Man Merle on my heels. Things had happened to me in these woods over the years—veiled threats from my demon father, attacks from a serial killer, animal attacks, ghosts and demons and death oh my! —and Merle had been ever the protector. I was almost guaranteed to have an occurrence of some sort passing through these trees, but it no longer scared me. I had embraced the abnormal, the supernatural, the evil and un-known. Mostly because I was all of the above.

Nothing scared me anymore. But it was mildly off-put-ting when I spotted the little girl standing in the middle of the path. I almost didn't see her, but the breeze picked up and ruffled her gossamer skirts, the fluttering soft pink a tarnish on the deep purple tones of the night woods.

"Hello there," I said.

I was answered by a high-pitched giggle coated in an asthmatic wheeze. First it came directly from the girl—body heaving, straining for air. Then trills of giggles came from the side of me, the branches above, the cemetery behind. Her laughter was a chorus with the crows; dissonant and haunting.

"Naw," I said. "Not today."

I strode forward, right up to the little girl. My talons burst from my knuckles, and I grabbed her on either side of her head and ripped her in two. A thick squelch echoed through the woods as flesh, muscle, and bone separated, with a final crack from her spine severing straight down the middle. I tossed her remains on either side of the path and would have just moved on if it weren't for the bugs.

The little girl had no blood, no ichor. Just bones and bugs, like the insects had consumed everything within the sausage casing that was her skin. I knelt, getting a closer look. They were beetles of some sort, with mottled roan shells, their bodies covered in fine hairs and scales. They were the size of pine roaches, if not larger, a good four centimeters at least.

I grabbed a couple of the beetles and stuffed them inside my vagina. I wanted to know what they were, more for curiosity's sake. This girl had been one of a myriad of ghosts I encountered on the regular—she was no more menacing, and not unique in her scare tactics.

But the beetles …

I'd consult the spirit of my friend, Miss Mojo when I got home. Or Google. Whatever I felt like when I woke from sleeping off this dirty night.

Chapter Two

Waking was a messy business. I never quite preferred the abrupt transition from night to sudden morning, a demand for me to get up and get at it for another day. Endless night was what I wanted; not death, but twilight and midnight, frog song and starlight. Instead, I got the abrasive rays of sunlight like pins trying to penetrate my eyelids, and the noise outside of a ruckus begun.

"Busy night?" Liza asked.

I groaned. Opened my eyes.

"Blurgahhhh," I mumbled, stretching the sleep from my bones.

Liza was a sight. A waking dream. Many times, I wondered if she was just that, a spirit that occupied my senses, my heart. Like New Friend. Or Friend. But other people could see Liza. She bought food at the market, went to the dentist, paid bills. She was flesh, but too good to be true.

And here I was, making a mess of not only her life, but

of her fancy sheets.

"Coffee's ready," she said, her delicate fingers already wrapped around a steaming mug. "Come. We can read on the porch a while."

I blinked long and heavy, and she was gone. I could have easily gone back to sleep, but there were things to do. Liza offered me patience for my escapades through the night, but I didn't want to push it by forfeiting our days.

I stood, and the silk sheets slid off me like water, revealing the mucky mess of my body. Dirt in every crevice, packed beneath my toenails and fingernails, and caked on the bedding in clumps. We had no carpet in the house, thankfully, so I could take care of my trail with a mop and bucket.

I started by hauling my ass into the shower. I scrubbed until my flesh was pink, and the water at my feet lightened from black to brown to crystal clear. I lathered my hair into a great foaming mass, massaged out the forest debris, and softened it with conditioner scented like honeysuckle and lavender. I took my loofah to the spots on my abdomen, foot, and wrist. The wormy marks were faint, but they remained, no matter how hard I scrubbed. They were itchy; maybe a little sore? Possible spider veins, varicose veins, or the like. Aesthetic aging bothered me. It meant less time left in a life where I'd already lost so many years. My entire childhood. But I supposed colourful veins, sagging breasts, and age spots were better than the alternative. Dead.

Once I was fresh and sparkling, I donned my bathrobe and swiped my hand over the steamy mirror. It was not my reflection. An old woman stared back.

"Friend," I said.

I hadn't seen her in oh, so long. Not since she'd disappeared inside her house after all that nonsense with Empusa. Not since Eden's Edge had come into my possession.

I'd aged, but not as much as she had. It had been ten years. She'd aged forty, at least. Maybe not aged. Decayed.

She was all blackened gums and milky eyes. Canyons of wrinkles etched a roadmap of life across her face, and her complexion was onion skin translucent, the curve and shadow of bone detailed and visible beneath the glow of the bathroom light.

"*Old* Friend," I said.

She belched, and globs of earthworms purged from her throat. One slithered out of her nose, and maggots writhed from the corners of her eyes.

"Here," I said. "Let me help."

I plucked a face cloth off the hanger beside the sink and got to work, washing my face—rather, the face in the reflection—tenderly sloughing away worms, dirt, and tears of maggots until Old Friend's face was just scars, wrinkles, and thin skin. I brushed her—my—teeth, exfoliating the black rot from her gums and the tar from her tongue, all while flossing the earth from between my teeth. Both of us had remnants of the cemetery in our maws.

I debated about getting back in the shower. Surely Old Friend's body was a mess, but I couldn't tell. It was a small mirror and didn't reflect anything below my collarbone. My own body, still toned with echoes of youth, had no remaining dirt or debris. I was clean enough. She was her own problem.

I left Old Friend in the mirror as I fetched clothes from the bedroom. The chill of winter lingered in the spring air, and there was nothing better than wrapping up in a hoodie and coffee. The coffee was hot, but not quite fresh. No mind. I tended to linger on the same mug for hours if I got lost in my own thoughts, which was an occurrence more regular than not. I poured coffee into a mug shaped like a large mushroom and stepped out onto the porch overlooking the back yard.

The morning dew was cool and wet on my feet. I rarely wore shoes or slippers, and this was why. I liked to feel the water on my soles, the dirt between my toes, sand and grit beneath my nails. In contrast, Liza's feet were fully armoured, contained in two pairs of woolen socks and crammed into a pair of black, fur-rimmed moccasins. Liza did not like the feeling of grime on her skin. She'd been exposed to enough filth for one lifetime.

"Beautiful day blooming," she said, jutting her chin to the rising sun.

To my right, a creak. A gargle. A groan.

Mary's eyes were trained on the same sunrise, though I couldn't be sure how she felt about it. Her rickety wheelchair was pushed right up to the edge of the porch, brakes on, block in front of her wheels. She couldn't move much on her own, but she had once tried to tip herself off the porch to the garden below. Had she wanted her head to smash off the decorative rocks Old Man Merle had hauled in as decor from the forest depths? Or was she simply trying to go for a jaunt in the fields like we did as children for the brief time we'd been friends?

Mary was no longer a child. She was confined to that wheelchair, speechless and damaged, no longer able to take care of any of her own needs.

Because of me.

"It's not your fault," Liza said with a sigh, seemingly reading my mind, exhaustion from this decade-old debate rising once again.

"Maybe I should have just let her die," I said. "Or killed her."

"I thought so at the time," Liza said.

"Do you still?" I asked.

"Is she dead just the same?" Liza asked.

She didn't expect an answer. This was just another prompt for reflection. Day after day for a decade we'd wheeled Mary around, propping her up alongside us and playing make believe that she was enjoying our escapades. Perhaps she was. Perhaps it was torture, a life worse than an end. Her body was a prison, and her mind … I had no idea what was happening in there. But if there was any possibility that I was giving her a second chance at life, I was going to continue to try. I was a witch. And a demon. With those powers, both beautiful and ugly, surely I could find a way to solve the puzzle that was Mary.

"Sit," Liza said. She patted the cushion beside her.

The porch swing creaked like old bones as I sat beside my love, curling my legs beneath myself and pressing into her side. Liza tilted her head, resting it on my shoulder. She was warmth to rival the rising sun.

"Another night in the woods," she said. A statement, not a question.

"No harm done," I said.

Well, there was the matter of my fingers. Despite my shower, my nail beds were still gritty, and the nails themselves clawed down to the quick. It wouldn't surprise me if one morning I woke up with bone poking through my fingertips.

"The sheets," she said.

"I'll wash them," I said, punctuating it with a sip of my coffee. "But first, caffeine."

We had a quiet day ahead, sheets not considered. There were no new residents at Eden's Edge, and the current ones were well established. I had intended to keep our little community quaint and simple and had managed to do that so far. There was a danger in what we had here, and I wanted to keep on top of that.

"I found more animals by the tent area," Liza said. "A couple marmots, an owl, and a pile of frogs."

I winced. A pile of anything was trouble, especially a pile of dead things.

"Did they look mauled?" I asked.

We had considered perhaps we had a feisty mountain cat on our hands, or a particularly murderous vulture.

"No," she said. "Just dead."

"Huh," I said. "I'll go clean them up after coffee."

"I believe Merle's on it," Liza said. "They were gone this morning."

Merle had followed me home last night, to ensure my safety. And he would have walked by the tent area on his way back. Merle was good that way, knowing what needed to get done and just doing it.

"We do need to stock the library," Liza said. "I want more books, and the last batch of campers took some of the more popular ones."

"Mmmm," I moaned into my coffee. "A trip to Chapters sounds delightful."

"Less romantasy, more sci-fi," Lisa said.

"Those romantasiers devour books," I said. "Let them feed."

In the distance, a raven let out a hearty gronk. His murder burst from the trees like a funnel of wind, sluagh on the hunt.

"Merle's bringing more firewood," I said, looking into the woods in the direction of the murder that had taken flight. "Kendra will run Evil Embers if we get more guests in this weekend. Even if we don't, she'll light the fire and tell stories to the ghosts."

The Beast, once a church and place of horrors when Eden's Edge was under the thumb of a cult leader and murderess, had succumbed to my razing many years ago. Now that patch of land was home to a large fire pit and sawed-off stumps for chairs, perfect for gatherings, singalongs, and late-night readings of horror tales illuminated by flame.

I had cleansed Eden's Edge without knowing that one day it would be my own. Liza and I turned Eden's Edge into a campground to earn some money. We had four cabins available to rent, and a section for tenting. We had a few buildings erected to use as a library, a common room, and a little general store, all of which were run by my old friend Marie. I'd met her at a campsite long ago, when Liza and I were on the run from ourselves. She'd happily relocated to Eden's Edge when I gave her the opportunity. Of that I was glad. Running a campground was something I was unfamiliar with, and I needed someone who understood who I was. What I was. And Marie did, because she, too, was a witch.

Liza laced her fingers through mine. Lifted her head and looked me in the eyes.

"Sheets, then let's go," she said. "Bookstore, and Costco for toilet paper and paper towels."

I nodded but didn't move. I was drowning in the black lake of her eyes, so full of pain and love and beauty. Her lips parted, revealing the white of her teeth and the gleam of her tongue. I kissed her, long and hard, and her grasp loosened, freeing my fingers. While I thread my fingers through her long, dark hair, her hand slid beneath the waistband of my sweatpants, the pads of her finger parting me, plunging. I moaned, my hips lifting into her touch. Another moan. Not mine.

Both our heads turned. Mary's head had turned as well, her black eyes aimed in our direction.

Liza jerked her hand out of my pants, and she scooted away from me.

So what if Mary saw? I wanted something to bring her back to life. Perhaps seeing and smelling the throes of passion might moisten her as well. Something, anything to spark a sign of life. Awaken a Mary that once was.

"Come on," Liza said, patting my leg. "I'll take Mary back inside, then we can get going."

Chapter Three

Traffic was thin, as it always was on a weekday. Normal people were at work. Normal people didn't receive inheritances and settlements from lawsuits from long-past trauma. Like traffic, the crowd at Chapters was sparse. Solo teens lingered in the graphic novel and dark academia sections, a small bible study group was huddled at a table in the inspirational corner, and a handful of people perused the flashy covers of the new release section.

Liza went to the coffee bar to grab us yet another dose of caffeine while I meandered through the fantasy section, my eyes drawn by the sprayed edges and intricate covers of coiled dragons and ethereal fae. I liked a good read of faeries fucking and warrior women, dragons scorching both earth and ex-lovers, but I 'd rather have been browsing the darker sections. Occult, witchcraft, alternate theology. Liza preferred I steer clear of those sections, though. I had a tendency to perseverate on books purporting to teach on subjects the authors had not lived. Liza suggest *I* pen a book. A how-to on witchcraft and demonology. A coupling of the two.

Instead, I distracted myself with fantastical tales of nonsense and make believe.

"Hello."

It was a small voice, not in my aisle. Obviously not speaking to me. People do not greet who they cannot see.

I touched the chrome crimson edges of a fantasy novel showcased on a table in my aisle.

"Hi," the little voice squeaked.

A tendril of my hair fluttered on my cheek, displaced by the breath of that voice. Odd, seeing as there was still no one in the aisle with me.

"Here," the voice said.

I rounded the corner into the next aisle. The horror section. There stood a little girl—the same little girl I'd seen in the middle of the night, in the middle of the woods.

"Hello there," I said. "I thought I tore you in half last night."

The little girl shrugged. "Don't know much about that," she said.

Her voice lilted with a slight accent I could not place.

Now that we shared an aisle, I could see that she was extending me a book. It was a thick tome with edges sprayed black, gold foil frogs adorning the spine.

I did not take the book from her.

"What's it about?" I asked.

"Witches," she said. "Many of them."

The fine hairs on my body stood at attention.

"Sounds like quite the story," I said.

"It's many stories," she said, her voice brimming with excitement. "One about a witch named Faelith, another about sister witches in the Dark Ages named Leaf and Tails."

"You like witches," I said.

"Aye," the girl answered.

"Me too," I admitted.

The little girl took a step toward me. I had to concentrate to keep my feet cemented in place. Why did I have the urge to recoil from a child? I took solace in the fact that she was enamored with the book in her hands, which is where all her focus lay. She fumbled through the pages and cracked the spine to spread the book out in front of me.

"Beautiful illustrations, as well," she said.

She was beaming. Which was odd, seeing as the picture was grotesque. Surely too much for the eyes of a child, though my own eyes had seen this very image many years before. It was a painting of fornication in a storm, a witch and a demon, his cock buried deep within her sex, so deep that he was splitting her in two. Her blood and his semen rained down, coating the faces of the people below. And those people choked on that slurry of fluids, their eyes and mouths wide with horror as they gawked at the scene above.

It was an illustration of Mom and Dad in the clouds, ripping themselves apart in waves of pleasure.

I touched the book and drew back. The glossy pages were wet with black blood. I sucked my finger. Salty. Tears, semen, maybe both. The plipping of the rain shower in that painting was all around me, a soft sound barely audible above the whir of the bookstore fans. The semen rain fell from the book … No, not from the book. From her, onto the carpeted floor of Chapters.

I pushed the book out of the way to gaze upon the puddle of red forming between the diamond made by the little girl's feet and mine. A lake of blood between us, obese drops of semen-thickened blood plip-plipping down to feed the growing puddle of fluid.

The girl was no longer intact. She was torn in two, each side wilted like soggy corn husks, exposing halved organs and splintered bones. One eye on each side of her face focused on me, giving her a cross-eyed expression that would have almost been funny had Sam Raimi concocted it on film.

One eye was hazy and glacier blue, the other black as night. Just like mine.

"Anna, Anna, quite contrary …" the little girl sang.

"Mary," I corrected her. "The lyrics are *Mary*, Mary, quite contrary."

"… how does your garden grow?" she continued, ignoring my correction.

She was rotting, this little girl. Decay had reached the marrow of her bones, the greenish sheen of old meat coating her organs and devouring the center of her spine. Dirt swirled through the blood and ichor, and those odd beetles feasted on intestines bursting with waste. Her skin was riddled with the veinish rot, just like mine, but hers was in great patches, not a tiny burst like on mine.

"… with burning hells and witches' spells …"

Her voice was off tune and wavering. Her vocal cords, now split in two, strained with visible effort.

"… and ravaged whores all in a row."

She was completely halved now. Both sides of her had peeled apart, drooping to the floor. With great effort, the sides slithered to standing, spaced a meter apart, and her arms lifted. Her head had fallen off in two halves, somehow severed at the neck, and she held them up for me to see. One hand was laced through light, curly hair. The hair clutched in the other hand was shiny, black, smooth.

Mary and Liza?

Their half-heads swung, their mouths agape, teeth sharpened to spikes, eyes hollowed. The wounds where their heads had been liberated were jagged, stretched, torn. Ripped off, not cut. Blood poured from Mary's head, while crystal clear fluid poured from Liza's.

I dropped to my knees between the girl's halves. Pressed my palms to the floor. Lowered my face to the carpet and lapped up Mary's blood. It was slick, warm, gritty. I pivoted, did the same with the pool of clear fluid from Liza's head.

Cool, briny. The carpet was rough, my tongue was raw from licking, and Liza's liquid stung the tender flesh.

Sea water?

"Tsk, tsk, tsk, tsk."

I sat back on my haunches. I was prepared to start explaining myself to whatever confused customer had just rounded the corner into the horror aisle, but it was no customer that stood there watching the display.

"Old Friend," I sighed with relief.

Her body was crooked and hunched, eyes white and gums black. She had her wispy white hair bundled in a haphazard bun atop her head, and her skin sagged from her bones like melted wax. She was naked, long breasts puddled on her thighs, translucent skin a window to the black veins beneath. Pus swirled with soil leaked from every hole, dribbling down her bright white thighs and pooling beneath her.

"What is all this, now?" I asked her, motioning to the two halves of the girl.

A cackle belched out of Old Friend's throat. She coughed, and a red feather purged from her mouth, fluttering in the air and landing on the little girl's shoulder.

"I'm tired, Old Friend," I said. "So tired. Of all of this."

The little girl spoke, her voice too brittle for someone so young.

"Then choose," she said.

I closed my eyes. The ocean heaved in my ears, the scent of kelp and salt heavy on my tongue. My skin tingled where the sun baked the water droplets on my flesh, and in the distance, a gull screeched.

"Wouldn't you like to see the ocean, when your life has been loam and thick brush?" she said.

Waves heaved my body. Seasickness gripped my guts, but the cool of the Pacific soothed me. A tentacle brushed my leg; kelp wrapped around my toes.

"Anna?"

I opened my eyes.

The ocean was gone, replaced by the scent of books and coffee. I was on my knees in the middle of the horror aisle, the surrounding carpet free of blood and fluids, the aisle devoid of any creatures other than myself.

"Anna?" Liza repeated.

I stood, brushed myself off, tucked a strand of my hair behind my ear.

"All good," I said. "Old Friend is with me. It's all good."

The look on Liza's face suggested she didn't believe a word I'd said. The re-emergence of any iteration of Friend was something we had talked about, something that she thought was a bad omen. Which it probably was. But oh, how I'd missed my Old Friend, despite what might be accompanying her back into my life.

"Sure," Liza said.

There was a stack of book cradled in her arm. I had yet to pick any. She no doubt wondered what I had been doing with my time.

"Got a call," she said.

She wasn't looking at me, but at the aisle around me. At the books, at the carpet. She wondered what had been there. What might still be there.

"A call?" I asked.

"Someone wants to come out to Eden and camp for the week," she said. "Some woman and her child."

"How did she find us?" I asked.

"Flyer at NA," Liza said. "Or AA. She wasn't clear."

I always wanted to help people in need. We offered brief respite in our cabins for people struggling with abuse, addiction, mental health issues. No safer place for them than a campground full of witches, demons, ghouls, and ghosts.

"Addict?" I asked.

"Would seem so," Liza said.

"Clean? Dry?"

"No idea," Liza said with a shrug. "She's at a program, so maybe?"

"Do we have anyone else booked this week?" I asked.

Liza shook her head. "Not until the weekend, and no cabins even then. Tenters and an RV."

"Good," I said.

Withdrawal was an ugly business. Campers with kids might not appreciate the process. But with empty cabins they could have their privacy. This woman and her child could ride out the worst without an audience.

"When would she like to meet?" I asked.

"As soon as possible," Liza said. "They're living out of her car. I did say we were in town today, so maybe …"

"Now?" I said.

I wasn't fucking prepared for this.

"Take your time and pick your books," Liza said. "We're meeting them in a couple of hours on the way back home. Gives us time to stop at Costco."

"Meeting where?" I asked, though I already knew.

"The diner," Liza said.

Behind her, Old Friend sighed, a cloud of red feathers escaping her lips as she did.

Chapter Four

I did not like the diner.

It was a fine enough place, but it was stained with memories. Were they bad memories? Maybe. But even bad memories are attached to good. They were all braided through each other, connecting time and experience into one big portrait of life.

The diner is where I first met Old Friend. Back then she was New Friend, headless, holding her bowl of blood. I remember her pretty little dress and shiny black shoes, the way she finger painted on the window in blood from her bowl.

We were sitting in that same booth now, Liza and I, on the same bench my mom and I had sat a lifetime before. There was an empty bench across from us, reserved for people waiting to find safety in Eden's Edge. First us, Mom and I, and now this mother and son.

"We're early," Liza said as she placed her hand on mine.

"I know," I said.

"You should eat," she said.

"A donut," I said.

The sweetness from that last donut I'd eaten as a child was like glass shards on my tongue. The sugar lingering there, just like it did when Mom was beside me all those years ago.

"You're nervous," Liza said.

"I'm tired," I said.

Old Friend was in the parking lot right outside our window. I put my palm on the glass, and she mirrored the movement, her hand contorted with arthritis and splattered with brown age spots over gnarled knuckles.

"Friend is here?" Liza asked.

"Old Friend," I corrected.

There was sadness in Liza's tone. Over the years, she had made peace with my eccentricities and my unusual friends, but it still unnerved her. She loved all of me, but parts of me were exhausting. I was an extension of her own past traumas.

"I'll go grab a couple donuts," Liza said.

When she shimmied over and stood, the red vinyl booth squeaked, and her boots crunched on the floor. Everything was so loud…

Why is it so loud?

And why does it sound like that?

I leaned over to look at the floor, expecting gravel or a broken plate where she'd stepped, but the floor was clean and shiny.

The crunching continued even after Liza reached the counter, too far for me to hear the sound of debris under her heels.

Tap tap tap went Old Friend on the glass.

I straightened up in my seat and met Old Friend's milky gaze.

Her finger, a too-long, crooked talon, tapped the glass again to ensure my attention. I watched as she produced a couple of large rocks from the gravel parking lot. Her mouth opened, jaw unhinging, and she sprouted new teeth. Normal teeth, white and straight and strong.

"Don't," I said.

But she did. She held a rock in her hand like an apple and bit down. The sound it made was like Liza's boots on a broken plate. Old Friend bit into that rock until her teeth fractured and chipped, exposing rotten roots. Shards of white porcelain splintered and hit the window like hail, *ping ping ping*ing and still she chewed, smashing her molars to bits. She threw that rock over her shoulder, bent, and appeared in the window again, this time holding a rock that didn't belong. Smoothed by water, slick with algae, rippled with blues, greens, and whites. She bit into this rock and the rest of her teeth cracked and fell from her mouth. What stubs of former teeth remained in her mouth were pushed into her gums as she bit down, until seeping holes were all that remained. She disposed of the rock by swallowing it whole. It stayed in her throat, a bulge straining the folds of skin hanging below her chin.

"Anna," Liza said.

I pretended to be looking out the window at the scenery. The trees, the birds fluttering about the brush, the cars in the parking lot. I calmed myself and turned to Liza. She stood at the head of the booth with a donut, but also with two people. A jittery woman with strings of greasy hair framing the pocked skin of her face, and a child. A boy who looked to be about eight or nine years old. Unlike the woman, he was tidy and clean, save the mop of unkempt ginger curls atop his head.

"Hello," I said. I offered a smile, not too large but detectable. I didn't want to show teeth; not yet. I didn't know if these two required a predator.

"Anna, this is Ursula," Liza said.

The gaunt woman extended a hand, which I took with

great caution. Her nails were chewed deep and bloody, and her fingers were stained yellow from nicotine and other burning abuses.

"And her son," Liza continued. "Aamon."

Aamon did not extend his hand. He looked at his shoes. I wondered if he was assessing how swift his sneakers were, and if he ran, would they carry him fast and far enough to escape us, Ursula, this diner, and his life.

"Sit," I said, motioning to the bench seat across from me.

They sat, Liza beside me, and Ursula and Aamon across from us.

"Ursula, like Mother Shipton," I said.

Ursula's eyes widened, further exposing the whites of fear.

"Huh?" she said.

"Ursula Southeil," I clarified. "English witch from the early 1500s. A prophetess and soothsayer. Turned men who displeased her to stone."

Ursula cocked her brow and half laughed, unsure if this was for real.

"I know a lot about witches. Obsessed since I was Aamon's age," I said, dipping my chin at Aamon.

"Oh, I ain't no witch," Ursula said. "Maybe my momma named me after that there fat one from under the sea. Momma liked cartoons and singin'."

"Why not name you Ariel, then?" Liza asked.

"I was born blue," Ursula said. "On account of the drugs. Hers, that is. My momma didn't like me none. Didn't think I was no royalty or pretty or nothin' like that. More like that fat witch than a pretty mermaid."

Aamon's hair was flaming ginger. More Ariel than Ursula.

"An interesting one, there," I murmered, studying Aamon. "Also, skin of blue. A Grand Marquis of Hell,

Aamon."

"Anna." Liza's voice was stern. A warning. She placed her hand on mine and squeezed until her knuckles turned white.

"Not meaning to scare you," I said. "There's time for discussion later. First, you are here because you need a place to stay."

Ursula squirmed in her seat.

"You are safe to feel uncomfortable with me," I said. "Cry, rage, laugh. Emotions are healthy. Human. Lean into it. I'm here to help."

"I'm an addict," Ursula said.

Clearly.

Maybe ...

"I ain't got no place to go," Ursula said, her lip trembling. "I ... I done things. And my boy ..."

Outside the window, Old Friend held up her hand. I mirrored the motion, aiming my open palm at Ursula to stop her.

"We can hash details later," I said. "Anyone is welcome to camp at Eden's Edge. Especially people who need to hide or heal."

Like someone had slapped her across the face, Ursula froze, eyes wide, then started sobbing.

Liza tended to that. She slid off the bench and guided Ursula to her feet, embracing her and leading her to the restroom where she would calm her, dry her tears, splash cool water on her face. Liza was good at comfort.

Years ago, my mom had to dry her own tears in that very bathroom. I remember her returning to the table with the fluff of toilet paper still on her face, her eyes red and puffy.

Aamon spoke, his voice startling me out of my memory.

"You gonna hurt us?" he said.

His voice was very small.

"No," I said. "Unless you hurt us."

Aamon's eyes were still low, focused on his lap.

"You want a donut?" I offered.

I was no good with kids. I had never really been one myself.

Tap tap tap.

Old Friend tapped the window with her talon. The toothless hole that was her mouth was filled with bloody crumbles of rock.

Aamon's head rose. He looked at Old Friend. His eyes were stormy grey and shining with tears.

"She won't hurt me?" he asked.

Could he see her?

No, he was just looking out the window.

Wasn't her?

"No," I confirmed. "I won't hurt you. No one will at Eden's Edge."

"You won't hang me up on the wall like Laz?" he asked, the pitch of his voice rising, the volume crescendoing.

"What?" I said. "I—"

"And chain me there while you rape her," he said, hysteria taking over, "her panties torn. Bloody and stained, just like her labia and asshole?"

Bats erupted in my belly, and my throat filled with sand. Panic and terror.

"I can still feel him inside me," Aamon said. "Tearing me open where little boys should not be torn. My bones, sticking out like cracked sticks. When he kisses me, I taste both my blood and hers."

"Hers?" I asked. Now it was my lips that were trembling.

Aamon jutted his chin toward the restroom. Toward Liza.

Those grey eyes turned a stormy black, his lips stretched into a grimace, his freckles darkening to spatters of blood. The diner dimmed and the noise crescendoed. The cracking of teeth on rocks, the flurry of birds taking wing, the crackle of wood on fire, the violent whoosh of waves against a rocky shore.

The restroom door opened, and Liza appeared with Ursula.

The diner was quiet and bright again. Aamon was looking down at his lap, sniffling.

"All good," Liza said as she ushered Ursula into the booth. "Well, as good as can be expected."

Ursula had calmed. Like Mom those many years ago in this same diner, her face was dotted with tiny pills of toilet paper. Her eyes were red and swollen.

"Can we come now?" Ursula asked. "To your campground?"

I nodded. I couldn't speak. Liza looked at me, stared expectantly.

"They'll follow us in their car," Liza said slowly.

I nodded.

Outside the window, Old Friend cried, bloody black tears filling the riverbeds of her wrinkles. Black rot had started to form on her pale feet, moving up her calves like capillaries.

"Okay," I said, though nothing was okay. "Let's go."

Chapter Five

Eden's Edge was in the same place as it always had been, but it was like I was making the trip for the first time again. Same darkness, same gravel road into the middle of the woods, same distance—four songs deep down a single-lane path. When I was little, I had ridden in the backseat. New Friend had been beside me with her bowl of blood sloshing on the windows and seats.

This time, Old Friend sat in the middle of the back seat. There was no blood, but infection seeped from her pores, and blood and feces dribbled from between her legs, staining the upholstery. She looked too old for menstruation, but certainly old enough for incontinence. Thankfully, I was the only one that could see or smell her. She needn't feel shame. I paid no mind to the realities of aging.

I wondered about Aamon and Ursula. Should she be driving? Was he in the backseat just as I was when I was his age? Did he, too, have a Friend holding a bowl of bodily fluid?

"All good?" Liza asked.

She was driving. My mind was too busy to focus on the road. We hadn't said one word since leaving the diner. Liza was good about giving me time to process. She knew that my world was busier than hers, with the sounds, sights, and scents of Others cluttering my senses. Lately, though, the veil seemed to be thinner. More noise, more impossible things transpiring around me. It was wearing on me, so I must have been wearing on her.

"Not sure," I said. "Something's wonky."

Liza chuckled. A calming sound.

"If your life wasn't wonky, I'd be worried," she said.

It wasn't an insult. Liza loved me for exactly who and what I was.

"This doesn't feel right," I said, meaning Ursula and Aamon.

"Then it's probably not," she said.

Her face strained. She would never say she was upset, or scared, or worried. But she was. If Ursula was a criminal like Allison had been, or her son dangerous, Liza knew I'd be on top of it. I would rip them to shreds before I ever let anything happen to Liza or Eden's Edge. But that didn't mean it wasn't going to be horrific. Traumatic. And Liza was full up on trauma.

"He knows about Laz," I said quietly to the floor mats.

The vinyl on the steering wheel tightened beneath Liza's grip. Her mouth drew into a straight line, and she breathed hard and heavy through her nose.

The last time Liza saw Laz, our childhood friend from our brief time together at Eden's Edge when it was run by a mad woman, he'd been chained to a wall, violated, his head lolled to the side in awkward death.

"No," she said. "Aamon doesn't know about that. No one does. It's impossible."

Liza knew full well that nothing was impossible. But I

let it be, especially since I'd prefer that she didn't pilot the car into the nearest tree or the next oncoming truck.

Finally, the trees parted, revealing Eden's Edge. It was different than it was when I was a child. I had ensured that. Old Man Merle and his workforce of ghouls had erected a row of log cottages, each strong but haphazard and random in their beauty. Miss Mojo and Marie had decorated with their own touches, including chimes made of bones and glass, dried flowers, creeping vines, and carved totems. The Beast was gone, replaced by a giant campfire and surrounding log seating. There was no need for a church or school in Eden's Edge. There was a library house, as there was in the original Eden, but this one was twice the size. Liza and I kept it well stocked, and Kendra—a demon I met a few years after I'd acquired Eden's Edge—kept track of the books. I was lucky enough to have picked up Kendra in my travels. She was an avid reader, and intensely knowledgable on literature and pop culture. I did have to polish her people skills a bit, which was not surprising seeing as I'd found her at an abortion clinic eating fetal matter out of waste containers. Ghouls will do that. Also, to keep her presentable to the living campers, Kendra had fashioned herself a body out of sewn-together hides and human skin. I did not ask where she'd got those, but after slapping a wig on her, she looked half presentable. Passable as human. Almost.

Liza pulled the car into the small lot we'd designated at the west of the campground. The area wasn't big enough for people to need vehicles to get around, and the quaint pathways and abundance of nature was part of the charm of being secluded in the woods. If people had loads to carry, like tents and stoves, we had a couple of electric golf carts available to mosey around on.

Ursula pulled her car next to Liza's, rolling a little too far and bumping a tree. She was rattled. Aamon sat beside her in the passenger seat, dead eyes staring straight ahead. I went to their car as Liza retrieved a golf cart to haul our stuff.

"Here," I said, opening Ursula's door for her. Her hands were still on the steering wheel. "Come. We'll load your stuff and take you to your cabin. It's small, but it's safe and clean."

"I … money …" Ursula stammered.

"Don't worry about that now," I said. "Let's get you settled away."

As Ursula got out of the car, I noticed scarring on her arms. Some fresh, some old and silver. Cuts. Bites. When she shut the car door, she flinched at the sound, even though she'd been the cause.

A deer. Skittish and hunted.

I didn't need to go to the passenger side to retrieve Aamon. He was standing at the boot of the car, luggage in hand by the time Ursula and I got there.

"Welcome to Eden's Edge," I said, more to him than to her. She wasn't in a state to hear anything.

"Can I look around?" Aamon said.

"You can," I said, "but it's late. There's no one around."

A lie. The ghouls and creatures were just rousing for the night.

"But can I explore?" Aamon asked.

"Of course," I said. "Would you like company, so you don't get lost?"

"I don't get lost," he said.

"I believe it," I said.

Beside me, Ursula started shaking. I took off my hoodie and slipped it over her head. She startled when I touched her.

"It's cold," I said. "Wear this tonight. Give it back tomorrow if you want."

Ursula didn't argue. She submitted to my gesture, a nonaction that unsettled me. This was a broken woman. She offered me a smile, which widened the caked cracks at the corners of her mouth. The shine of blood emerged, dark against the white and yellow crust of her lips.

"You need water and sleep," I said. "When we get to the cabin you're staying in, you will drink water and take a sleeping pill. It will knock you out for the night. We'll deal with the rest in the morning."

I'd have to have someone stand sentry. This woman was smack dab in the center of addiction. There was no telling what would happen if she freaked out in a strange place in the middle of the night. The marks on her arms suggested she was no stranger to self harm. Liza and I had Mary in the other bedroom of our cabin, so I'd get Miss Mojo to hang out and supervise. Ursula and Aamon wouldn't see her so they wouldn't feel unsafe.

Liza arrived with the golf cart, and we shifted Ursula and Aamon's belongings from their trunk to the cart. They didn't have much, and what they did have was contained in plastic grocery bags. We were just about loaded when Aamon snatched a bag from my hands.

"Mine," he hissed.

From what I could tell, the bag contained a jar. When I was little, my jar contained my father's heart. I wondered what was inside his jar.

"Come with us," I said to Aamon. "See where you live. Then you can go off on your own if you think you can find your way back."

"I can," he said. "I'm good with directions."

Ursula spoke, her voice coated in gravel and phlegm.

"He is smart," she said. "He is strong."

Gooseflesh rose on every centimeter of my body.

Those were words my mom had spoken to me many times.

We rode across the campground to an empty cabin across from Old Friend's home. I'd still never been inside Old Friend's place—not when she was New Friend, or when she was just Friend. It had survived the fire I started when I was a child and had stayed standing ever since. The door with the red knob was still locked for everyone but her, and the bowls with tears and blood remained full on either side of the banister flanking the porch at the top of the stairs. This is where Old Friend hopped off the back of the golf cart, her weight having no impact on the springs. Liza parked as I watched Old Friend disappear into her home.

"What's in that one?" Aamon asked, pointing there.

He can see it.

Not even Liza could see Old Friend's home. She never good, not even when she was New Friend. Liza knew to steer clear of that patch of land after I'd told her about it, but she never asked any questions. None of the campers had been able to see it, and neither had Marie, Mojo, or Merle. No one.

But now, Aamon could.

"An Old Friend of mine lives there," I told him.

"I like her cabin," he said.

"I do too," I said.

The four of us carried the bags inside, and I stocked the fridge and cupboard with some of the goods we'd purchased at Costco. It wasn't much, but enough to keep these two comfortable for a while.

"May I go now?" Aamon asked.

"Yes," I said. "Be strong and smart, like your momma said."

"Always am," he answered, his grey eyes swirling like a storm.

"No doubt," I said.

I nodded ever so slightly down the road, at the cloud of flies amassing there. They wouldn't take the form of a woman; not just yet. Not until (or if) Aamon and Ursula became aware of what, exactly, resided here at Eden's Edge. Miss Mojo would remain a cloud of flies and follow Aamon, ensuring his safety during his exploration.

Kaz walked around the cabin and stood beside me.

"They need watching?" he asked.

"She does," I said, motioning to the cabin. "Her son will wander. Mojo will follow him."

Kaziel still didn't realize he was dead, I don't think. I hadn't even realized it when he died in my arms a decade ago. But his role as mountie had followed him into the afterlife, and he made it his business to be the law of Eden's Edge. Even with his neck a gaping chasm and his cheek and jaw no more than shredded flesh and bone, he patrolled the property with diligence, alerting myself, Miss Mojo, or Old Man Merle to any untoward behaviour or odd goings on. He still hadn't figured out how to inflict restraint or damage upon other offenders, though.

"Is she going to be okay tonight?" Liza asked.

"Yeah," I said. "Kaz had already disappeared inside the cabin. "I have someone watching her."

Liza didn't ask who. It was still a lot for her to understand. She couldn't see Kaz, or Miss Mojo in her human form, or Old Man Merle. I'm not sure she wanted to.

"I'll walk home," I said to Liza.

"It's late," she said.

"I'm aware," I said. "Has she taken the sleeping pill?"

Liza nodded. "Two, actually."

"Risky," I said. "We don't know what else she has in her system."

"Judging by the twitching and trembling, I'd say she's stone cold sober."

"Perhaps," I said.

Liza knew better than to argue. I was a stubborn cunt on the best of days. She wanted me home, not galavanting about at night, but my wanderings were inevitable. Not even I knew how to stop them. At least this time my moonlight absence would have purpose. As Liza drove off with the golf cart, I ascended the steps and went inside Ursula's cabin.

Ursula was sitting on the couch, a pair of pantyhose

knotted tight around her bicep, working a needle into a bulging vein framed by an old bruise. Kaz was clawing at her arm, trying desperately to make purchase to keep that poison out of her veins.

"It's okay," I told him. "She's an addict. Just let me know if she seizes or gets sicker than an addict would."

Kaz nodded. Being a former officer on the streets of Vancouver, he was no stranger to addiction, overdose, and death.

"I'm sorry," Ursula mumbled. "I had to. It's cold, and my head … my skin was going to crawl off, and—"

I held up my palm, silencing her.

Once the heroin was pushed, Ursula let herself unfold onto the couch, needle still sticking out of her arm. Her eyes fluttered, her mouth loosened into a slack smile, and urine bloomed on the front of her jeans. I plucked the needle from her arm and dabbed the blood droplet that remained with a tissue from my pocket.

I watched her for a moment—the twitching, her scars, the filth that marred her every nook and cranny. Once her breathing grew heavy, I went to the kitchen and filled a bowl with warm water and grabbed a cloth from the drawer. She was a slight woman, all bones and little flesh, so it didn't take much to shimmy her out of her clothes. I moved her from the wet spot on the couch and carefully washed her, scrubbing away grime and cleansing the folds of her labia. After she was clean enough, I slipped a nightgown over her head and tilted her onto the two clean cushions of the couch, taking the third with me to wash.

I left all her her bags where she'd dropped them on the floor, knowing full well that they were stocked with all manner of drugs. She wouldn't kill herself, though. The odour of death was nowhere near. Ursula was chasing a high, nothing more. And she was too weak to make the final decision. As for accidental overdose, that was always a possibility, so I gave a sharp whistle through my teeth. A fluttering of wings, the soft smack of a body against the window, then Erinyes flew in through the door.

She always hit the window first. Hard to navigate the skies with no head.

My Mom's old familiar, Erinyes the cardinal, took her perch on the arm of the couch. Her body bobbed as if she were pecking lice from Ursula's fit of hair, her wing swiping away the puffs of dust motes as they were displaced from Ursula's tangles.

"Let her know if Ursula looks like she's in distress," I said to Kaz, and pointed at the headless cardinal. "She might not see it, but you will."

Kaz no longer needed sleep, so he could watch Ursula all night. Erinyes would retrieve me if anything went wrong. I might be able to save Ursula, I might not. But I'd sure as hell try.

I left, my hearts heavy as the crisp night air entered my lungs. I almost stumbled at the bottom of the steps but caught myself before face planting into the front garden.

A pile of frogs were arranged at the base of the steps. Had they been there when we entered? Not likely. Ursula wouldn't have noticed if there was a grizzly slumbering there, but Liza would have.

I dropped to my knees and picked the top frog off the pile. It was damp with death and bloated with rot. I gave it a gentle squeeze and gasses leaked out, deflating it in my grasp. I set him aside and picked up another, moving them out of the way of the step and counting as I went.

Twenty frogs in total, stacked neat and orderly. I wanted to go get Liza and ask if she could see them, or if this was just another of my peeks through the veil, but she needed rest. And a break, from everything, from me. So, I set the last frog off to the side and stood, then scanned the campsite. It was a weekday, so no other campers. The other three cabins were dark and empty, and the tenting area was all long grass blowing like blue hair in the moonlight. Merle would need to mow that before tenters arrived.

I would not sleep, so I walked, through the cacophony of nightsong and nature stirring, watching for whatever new Other had come to haunt me.

Chapter Six

I did not wake in the woods, because in order to wake, you'd first have to sleep. I was wound up with worry for Ursula, and also curious as to Aamon's whereabouts, but I did not search for him. Miss Mojo would keep an eye on him. Like Erinyes, she'd alert me if need be. Instead, I strolled around Eden's Edge until my footsteps padded in harmony with the sounds of nature, and stars speckled the sky like flecks of paint on an indigo canvas. Save the natural light from the moon, and the wane glow of my cabin in the distance, Eden was draped in darkness.

Children were playing. Their laughter replaced the daytime birdsong, just as sweet and lilting. Their music drew me in their direction, toward a patch of land where we had not built a structure. This was the spot where The Home once stood—a place where orphaned or stray children came to live during my childhood stay at Eden's Edge. Last time I'd seen these children, they were dead, blood spilled by Allison before I could liberate her head from her body.

Now, they were frolicking, translucent, chasing firebugs in the night. I clucked my tongue and they stopped. They turned to me, eyes solid black, mouths toothless, arms and legs too long, their bodies the color of bone. Ghosts of the children they had been yet still were.

"Play," I said.

They resumed their frolicking, leap frogging over one another, chasing in and out of the trees. Liza, Laz, Mary, and I had one time done the same thing, playing in the woods at night, exploring.

The wind ruffled my hair on my cheek, my split ends like spider's legs tickling my skin. I brushed it away, touching my cheek. My fingers came away wet with tears. My tears reminded me of my grief, and I followed it to the opposite end of Eden's Edge, to the bare patch of land that had once been Allison's home. I had burned that house and eaten the ash, devouring all the death to rid it of the predator and prey that found their end there.

But not everything could be cleansed.

"The children are playing," I said to Laz.

As was his way, he did not answer. He was hanging mid air—floatings, rather—chained to a wall that was no longer there, head lolled to the side. Exactly how he'd died.

"You could go play, too," I said.

Laz was screaming. I allowed myself to hear it, this noise that was constant if I didn't block it out. It was a hollow sound that bellowed out of his throat like a foghorn, a dissonant version of the hysterical screams he'd unleashed before his captor had ended his life to silence the wailing. I muffled that sound when I chose to, a skill for which I was grateful. Otherwise, I'd hear Laz's anguished wailing blasting over Eden's Edge all day and night.

Laz had been howling like that for thirty years.

I had to believe it was an echo. A film stuck on a loop, and that his pain and shame were not continuous, ongoing.

His body had stretched like taffy, his toes pert near touching the ground. His body was smooth, without bruising, without the prolapse, tearing, shattered and jagged bones as he'd been inflicted with as a boy. The waste that dribbled down his legs was gone, as were the soiled underwear. His tearful eyes were matte and solid black.

The torture and biological horror had passed. The trauma, though, remained, keeping him suspended midair, stuck in this loop. I hoped his mind had moved on. Seemed like it had. In all the years I visited him, he never responded to me. Not to my voice, my touch, the aroma of flowers or baked bread that I wafted under his nose. The other ghosts of Eden responded to all that stuff.

I hoped there was nothing left for Laz but empty flesh hanging in the air.

I sat a while with him, regardless, rubbing his foot, humming a melody over his screams. If it didn't comfort him, it comforted me. No one else could see him—not Liza, not Mary, and that was a relief. The last time Liza'd seen Laz, he was hanging raped and broken, fresh after she herself had been violated and maimed. She did not need to relive one second of that. And Mary. Mary, who had been closest to Laz, who had lived with him the longest at Eden's Edge, had no idea that he had even passed until I told her. I didn't give any details other than he was gone and in peace. A half-lie. Thankfully, no one could hear him scream but me. Not even Merle, Miss Mojo, or Kaz. His existence was known by me alone.

When it was time to go, I kissed Laz on the hand. I don't know if he felt it, but I always did that. For me, maybe for him.

I silenced Laz's voice in my head as I walked away from Allison's former lot. The scent of lilacs and sweetgrass sweetened the air, and even in the dead of night, the buzzing of the bees played like a bow on strings. My throat started to burn. I cleared it, and stabbing pain shot through my neck and jaw.

I clutched my neck and heaved. I coughed and sputtered and covered my mouth to dampen the sound. I didn't want to rouse Liza, Marie, or Ursula.

My coughing subsided, and I lowered my hand. It was wet, but this time not with tears. Even in the spare light of the waning crescent moon I recognized the black of blood at night. I swallowed, and the inside of my throat crackled like breaking bones. Then another crack, louder, bigger. Behind me.

I turned and saw two eyes glowing in the night. Bright, white, unblinking. Maybe a mountain lion, hunched and ready to pounce. It was in the middle of the lane, enveloped by shadows.

"Psssppspp," I hissed at it.

It didn't move. The noise I made caused another coughing fit that sounded like the clattering of bones in a mason jar. I tried to keep an eye on the cat as I hacked and hacked, but I couldn't catch my breath, and my chest hurt, and …

The cat charged, closing the gap between us in long, rickety lopes. When it came closer, I saw it was a she, and not a cat at all. It was Old Friend, long breasts dragging on the ground as she galloped toward me on all fours, her eyes glowing white and mouth pulled into an oozing black snarl.

Would she kill me? I didn't believe so. Did she have control of herself? I was unsure.

Old Friend pounced and landed with her knees square on my belly, knocking the wind out of me. I coughed, that sound of bones rattling crescendoing, wheezing out of me in snaps and gargles. Old Friend readied herself, pushing her body against mine before jumping in the air once more, landing with enough force to snap my lowest ribs.

That did it. Whatever was caught in my esophagus shot out of my throat and landed with a splat against Old Friend's cheek. She grabbed the object, rolled off me, and sat on her haunches beside me while I caught my breath.

"That hurt," I whispered. Volume hurt.

I didn't fault Old Friend for the pain. I realized she was doing the Heimlich to save me. I rolled on my side, then up to sitting. Old Friend was huddled over with the object in her hand, licking it and stroking it with a bony finger.

"May I see?" I asked.

At first, she growled and hid it from me, tucking it to the side. I held my hand out and waited patiently, then after a few minutes she relinquished her new treasure. It was hot and soft in my hand, a clot bigger than my esophagus or my trachea. I smeared the blood and viscous snot with my fingers, clearing it away to see the object beneath. Turned it in my hand and held it up to my face.

Fur. Brown and wet. Two black eyes. The protruding yellowed bone of a snapped neck.

A squirrel's head.

"Gus?" I said.

Indeed, it was Gus. I'd recognize his little face and whiskers anywhere. The last two times he'd come out of me he'd exited through my vagina when I'd birthed him as my familiar. This time, I'd expelled him in a goopy mess that restricted my air and resulted in some broken ribs. And a broken neck, for him.

"Where's the rest of your body, little dude?"

I hated to think that I'd have to purge the rest of him like I had his head. Vaginal birth had been way better.

"Why did you come out that hole?" I asked.

My gaze lowered to Old Friend, who was still on her haunches beside me. Her knees were dropped to the side, her bruised and drooping labia dragging in the dirt as she rocked side to side.

"Yeah," I said. "We're too old for birth, I suppose."

The inside of my throat and sinuses still burned with sick, so I cleared my throat and snorted. Snot clogged my nose, so I pressed one nostril and blew. A thick booger came half out. I pinched it between my fingers and pulled. It shifted deep in my sinuses, tugging and tearing as I extracted it from my nose.

"One leg," I said, pinching Gus's dismembered limb between my fingers.

A few more snots and blows, and I evicted two more legs from my nose.

"Three limbs accounted for," I said.

The sheepish look on Old Friend's face and the way she pinched her lips into a tight line told me everything I needed to know.

"Drop it," I said.

I held my hand out, and Old Friend let her jaw hang slack overtop my palm. Gus's final leg—the front left—spiraled into my hand on a web of drool.

"All accounted for," I said. "Body and tail notwithstanding."

That was a problem for another time.

Old Friend hissed at me and spun on her heels. She scampered away on all fours, disappearing between the cabins with grunts and groans. I cradled Gus's remains in my hands, massaging them.

I'd put him in a jar or eat him. Something to keep him with me. Death was natural in nature, but I knew this wasn't a simple case of the loss of a familiar. When Friend appeared, Gus followed, and chaos would ensue. I knew that like I knew my own body. Like I knew Mom's face and the bitonal growl of Dad's voice. Like I knew Liza's curves and the taste of her sweat.

Something was brewing in Eden's Edge.

Chapter Seven

As anticipated, I did not sleep. Not a wink. I did stare at my ceiling, finding creatures in the patterns of the stucco. Occasionally my mind would zone out in an attempt to rest, but my head filled with a medley of past traumas. Mary's eyes as Allison and Bobbie drove away with her. The sight of my mom's slit throat. My own talons piercing the soft skin on my dad's belly. The stench of Bobbie Pickton's pig farm.

And amongst that familiar barrage were new smells, sounds, tastes. The cackling of a flock of Wild Hunt, the mournful cry of a single cello, the stretching of skin.

I turned my gaze from the ceiling and caressed my blanket, trying to ground myself back into reality. My fingers penetrated dirt. My blanket was loam and clay, soft and cool. The air was thick with the stench of blood and burning excrement, with undertones of lilac and moss.

I forced my eyes opened and stood. I ignored every one of my senses and got into the shower. The more I scrubbed,

the more the foreign sensations went away. I wasn't dirty—
I'd had no overnight escapades in the cemetery, after all—but
I scrubbed myself raw anyway. If I could have scrubbed in-
side my throat, ears, and nose, I would have.

The black veins on my skin had spread. Or had they?
With shower water running over my eyes, the three spots
seemed bigger. And now there was a fourth. I almost missed
it, but it caught my eye when I was washing under my breast.
It was on the underside of my breast near my armpit. A lymph
node? Cancer?

No. I couldn't think about that.

Once I was done, I closed the faucet and breathed in the
remaining steam. Everything still tasted, sounded, and felt
foul. Panic threatened to take hold. I needed Liza. The presence of people and the expectation of social performance often alleviated my symptoms of anxiety. I pulled the shower
curtain to the side and stepped out of the tub. A candle flickered on the counter. I hadn't lit a candle. It was morning, and
the sun was bright.

I rubbed my eyes and blinked hard one, two, three times.

Aamon was standing in my bathroom. The door was
shut, and there he was, on the wrong side of it. On the *inside*,
where my body was on display and my nerves were frayed.

"Hello there," I said.

"Hello," he answered.

The stick of a lolly hung out of his mouth like a fag. The
sweet aroma of the sugar was potent, overpowering the former stench I'd experienced when I'd awoken.

"I am naked," I said.

"I see," he said.

I didn't get uncomfortable very often, but this was unpleasant. Aamon's shorts bulged with his swelling hardness,
an off-putting reaction from someone who was supposedly
just shy of ten. But I didn't cover myself. I toweled off, ran a
comb through my hair, put some lotion on my face, then faced

the boy once more.

"Get out," I said.

Aamon cocked his head and smiled.

He was blocking the bathroom door.

"At least out of the way," I said.

He shook his head. His smile widened, his teeth bearing down on the lolly stick until it snapped. The freed half hit the floor and squiggled toward my feet. I didn't move. The stick was an albino millepede greyed with decay, leaving a crimson trail as it slimed onto my foot.

"Why are you here?" I asked Aamon while watching the worm ascend my shin.

His answer was a melody from deep in his guts. More church organ than voice, it came out in a minor key, baritone rumbles that shook the flickering flame on the counter.

"*Me*," he growled.

The millipede continued its climb until I felt the wisp of its feet on my labia. It was a finger parting my lips, finding its entrance, squirming inside me and settling in my uterus. My right breast throbbed in pain and curdles of yellow leaked from my nipples onto the floor.

"Out," I said, but my breath came as a huff of air rather than a word.

I doubled over; my guts wracked with cramps. Thick, spoiled milk poured from my nipple as clear fluid gushed from the apex of my legs. I bore down, hoping for Gus's tail and body, but when I placed my palm between my thighs, it came to rest on a soft globe of flesh.

"Out," I said. I was unsure if I was talking to Aamon or the thing inside me.

One more clench and push, and the thing dropped from me to the floor.

The pain ceased, the fluids dried up, and on the floor between my feet was a pink bundle of flesh, black and white fuzz covering its head.

"A baby," I said, and Aamon said it in unison.

"Baby," we repeated as I picked the infant off the tile and cradled it in my arms. It was a girl … and a boy. Behind a swollen set of testicles was a puffy little labium. Matched the duality of the rest of the baby—half a head of blonde hair, half ginger. One white eye, one black. I looked over at the mirror, at my own face. I had a glacial blue eye and a pitch black one, a change that'd happened soon after Liza and I had moved back to Eden's Edge.

My baby.

The millipede was attached to the baby's belly button, the other end reaching deep inside of me and still pumping nutrients. With the baby secured in one arm, I fished in the bathroom drawer for a pair of shears. When my hand closed around them, I made two smooth, sudden moves—I cut the umbilical millepede, then drove the closed shears into Aamon's eye, straight into his brain until it tapped the back of his skull.

The baby wailed. Aamon dissipated into a whorl of bloody steam.

A knock at the door.

"Anna?"

Liza opened the door.

I stood in the center of the bathroom brandishing the shears like a weapon, my other arm empty, cradling nothing against my throbbing breast.

Liza's eyes were wild with the desire for flight. She was that little girl again, climbing out of Allison's basement window and fleeing into the woods, into a youth full of abuse, poverty, and pain. She backed up and shut the door.

"Liza, I—"

"Ursula and Aamon are here," she said through the closed door. "I'll feed them and give them something to sip on while you get yourself together."

"Aamon?" I said.

"Uh, yeah," she said. "The little boy from last night. In cabin four."

"I know, but … he's here?" I asked.

"Yes," she said. "Downstairs. I gave him a Pop Tart about ten minutes ago. I thought you'd be down, but …"

Liza trailed off. The blade in my hand was dripping blood—Aamon's blood and the blood of the cord—but of course Liza hadn't seen. Because Aamon was never up here. His eye was downstairs, completely intact, looking at that Pop Tart.

"I'll be quick," I said.

Liza's footsteps padded out of the bedroom and toward the kitchen.

I rinsed the sheers off in the sink for good measure and surveyed the bathroom. No one there but Old Friend, who was sitting on the toilet, afterbirth dangling from her vagina into the water.

"You saw the whole thing?" I asked.

Old Friend smiled and cried. In her arms she was rocking something, cooing at it in grandmotherly tones, waggling her finger in front of it. Whatever she held shivered and shook as Old Friend hummed a lullaby.

"Give it," I said.

With a scowl and quick chattering of her teeth, Old Friend relinquished her treasure.

"Oh," I said as I took the spine and attached ribs from her.

I'd birthed the rest of Gus.

In the bedroom, I unscrewed the top of the mason jar on the windowsill and poured the contents onto the dresser. Gus's head rolled to a stop, and I aligned the spine with the splintered bone at the back. Once the legs were each put in place, the bones snapped together and Gus stood. He shook and stretched, them scolded me with a string of shrill chirps and chatters.

"Hey," I said. "Not my fault. We're all of us aging."

His head and legs were fuzzy and full, but his body was bones. And still no tail.

I dressed, my nether region still throbbing from the trauma of birth, my breast still dripping with food for a babe that didn't exist. I'd birthed Gus twice before, but this was different. Before it had been Gus and only Gus. And I'd been alone. Well, not quite alone. Something from beyond the veil witnessed all that madness. Old Friend and … whatever Aamon was. Or something masquerading as him.

I was about to leave the bedroom when I spotted something out the window in the backyard. A body. Human? No. There was fur, and a bloated belly that did not rise with breath. Paws. Possibly a mountain lion. It wasn't Old Friend this time. She was still sitting on the toilet in the ensuite. The grass was wet with morning dew, but still, I could see the blood splatter marring the lawn's blades.

The cat wasn't there. Or it was; I had no idea. I didn't care. All I could think of was the baby, and a fierce yearning to protect it. To protect me, and Liza, and Eden's Edge. Eden was all I had; all I ever had. Only now did I know who and what I was, and I'd never had a home like this. I yearned to start over in Eden's Edge as it is now, with no Allison, with all my knowledge of witchcraft and the occult, and Liza by my side.

"Mourning my childhood?" I pondered aloud.

That didn't feel quite right.

"Anna?" Liza called from far away.

The cat could wait. The baby wasn't real. And we had a momma and her boy here that needed my help.

Chapter Eight

Aamon was sitting at the table, nibbling on the corner of his Pop Tart when I appeared in the kitchen. He had barely eaten anything other than a few crumbs off the edges.

"Change is difficult," I said, eyeing him as I poured myself a coffee. "I didn't much want to eat when I first got here, either."

Liza was in the living room with Ursula, sitting beside her on the couch.

"He's already had two," Liza said. "That's his second two."

Aamon took another nibble, the strawberry sprinkles tinkling down onto his plate as he chewed.

"Ah," I said.

I left the boy to his sweets.

"And you," I said as I lowered myself into the chair across from the couch. "Have you eaten?"

Ursula was trembling. The corners of her mouth were

cracked and yellowed, and white lines of dried drool striped her cheek. At least she'd slept. But she looked weak and sickly, with patchy hair and skin the colour of dry river rocks.

"Can't," Ursula said. "Sick."

The effort of speaking caused Ursula to heave, a damp belch escaping and filling the room with the stench of old food and bile.

"Soup then," I said. "Bone broth. If you like, I can put it in a mug, and you can sip it. But you must get something into your system, or you'll only get worse."

Ursula nodded. I don't think she agreed, but she hadn't the energy to argue or refuse.

"Normally," I said, "we'd discuss the particulars of your stay here, but I don't think you have the capacity to be an active participant in any planning right now. So, I'm going to set you up to get healthier, and we'll revisit specifics when you're in a right state of mind."

Ursula broke down. Her bony shoulders heaved as she sobbed, and she tangled her hands in her hair, pulling until her scalp turned white. I moved across to sit beside her and guided her hands out of her hair and into her lap.

"That hurt is okay," I said, "but you've already pulled out a good deal of hair. You know what else works?"

Ursula sniffled, but her sobbing had calmed.

"Here," I said.

I stood slowly, so as not to startle Ursula. Addicts were like deer on an eternal night highway, everything and everyone around them being engines and headlights. I went to the curio cabinet behind the couch and fumbled through its many small drawers until something poked my finger.

"Ah," I said. "Here."

I returned to the couch with my hand cupped. I sat beside Ursula and held out my palm.

"Careful now," I said. "It's sharp."

I dropped the dark, star-shaped seed into her palm. She

closed her hand around it and grimaced.

"Goathead," I said. "Also known as Devil's Thorn. We find it mostly around the Okanagan, though it's not native to here. It's a nasty, noxious weed, but these seeds serve some good."

Ursula loosened her grip to bring the seed up to her face. She rolled it around in her hand and winced.

"I've seen people and … other things … from all walks—mental illness, addiction, grief," I said. "I understand that physical pain is easier to deal with than emotional pain, but I want you to be safe. Use this instead of pulling at your hair." I glanced at her arms, at the silvery lines there. "Or cutting. When you were younger?"

Ursula nodded. "And recently."

There were fresher scars there, ones that she blocked from view by wrapping her arms around herself.

"There are other, safer options," I said. "Use the goathead. Squeeze it in your hand, roll it on your legs, abdomen. Do not put it inside yourself or we'll have to deal with extraction and infection. If it doesn't sate the need to self harm, let me know. I will allow you to do what you need, but safely. I can sterilize the blade for you, at least."

Ursula's face was slack with shock.

"We don't judge here," I said. "Be who you are. You are safe, and you are strong."

Tears rolled down her cheeks once more, but they were peaceful. A relief.

I patted her leg. "You stay here and rest," I said.

I stole a glance at Liza, who dipped her head in acknowledgement.

"Liza will stay with you and get you some of that bone broth. I made it myself. Moose, so lots of protein. Drink it, then drink some more. I want you sipping it all day."

"Okay," Ursula said. Her voice was still small but growing steady.

"Later, we'll give you something to help with any pain or tummy troubles," I said, "but not until you have some food in your system."

"You have your own pharmacy?" she asked.

"Of sorts," I said. "I'll explain later."

"Where are you going?" she asked.

She'd shifted closer to me on the couch. The outside of her thigh was almost touching mine. Already, she felt safe. That's good.

"Aamon and I are going exploring," I said.

With that, the young lad's ears perked. He jumped out of his chair, nearly upsetting his now-empty plate.

"Do you have a playground?" he asked.

"We sure do," I said.

"Couldn't see nothin' last night," he said. "There was lots and lots of bugs. And there was a weird old dude by the big bonfire pit."

"He feels safe there," I said. "His friends are there."

Miss Mojo was the bugs Aamon saw. And she didn't stray far from the site of The Beast where she had taught for many years. She and Old Man Merle congregated there most days and nights, cracking their jokes and weaving their yarns. But Merle, in death, had been unseen by all living eyes but mine. A ghoul for only someone like me. And, apparently, Aamon.

"Come then," I said.

Aamon came. He didn't trail along like a lost puppy, but barreled ahead of me, beating me to the bottom of the front steps and turning left.

"Other way," I said.

"What's this way?" he said continuing on his path.

"The entrance," I said. "You leaving?"

"Not yet," he said.

Aamon was confident and smart. I scolded myself for interpreting it as arrogance. I came off as abrupt and arrogant as a child, but it was power and curiosity. In my older age, though, that confidence had waned. I longed for my mom's words, yearned for her guidance.

You are smart. You are strong.

Aamon had no guidance, and his mother gave no strength. I'd have to have enough for all.

Aamon cranked a u-turn and was now strutting by my side, kicking pebbles down the gravel path with his worn converse.

"Are you a witch?" he asked.

"Yes," I said.

"Are there other witches here?" he asked.

"Not just witches," I said. "Others. Witches, ghouls, ghosts … demons."

"My momma ain't no witch," Aamon said.

"Perhaps she's a demon," I suggested.

"Uh uh," he said. "She's just a junkie."

Wow. Little prick.

"A junkie is many things," I corrected. "A fighter, a winner, a survivor. She's healing."

"Is this rehab?" Aamon asked. "Cuz she's done that before. Didn't take."

"This isn't rehab," I said.

"But why are we here?" Aamon pondered.

"Your mom found us," I said. "Advertisement at a meeting. Perhaps she was drawn here. Perhaps this is where you are both meant to be."

Aamon's brow scrunched. He was considering this possibility.

"I have lived here for many years," I explained to Aamon as we walked, the gravel crunching beneath our shoes. I sauntered slow. My story was not short. "I came here to be rescued as a girl and it turned out it was I who needed to do the rescuing. I returned as an adult and decided my lot in life was to pay it forward."

"Rescue people from this place?" he asked.

"*With* this place," I said. "When I was little, I was lost. I thought I was a witch, but I saw dark things. My powers were unclear, my reality skewed. This place taught me much about myself, but my stay was short. I tried to avoid myself for many years, but when I moved back here, I embraced the parts of me I was hiding from."

"The brooms and spells?" he asked, his eyes twinkling saucers.

"My relationship with power and death," I said. "I am demon, I am witch …"

Half-breed tainted, rotten bitch.

… "I have studied many years, through literature, experimentation, conversing with my peers and loved ones."

"Other witches and demons?"

I nodded. "Ghouls, ghosts, and animals, too."

His pace had quickened with excitement, but he didn't leave my proximity. He buzzed around my legs like a hummingbird.

"Can you do magic?" he asked. "Show me!"

"It doesn't work like that," I said. "I do what needs done, when it needs done. Not even I know what that might be until it happens. And I see things, hear things. Creatures, echos, ghouls and ghosts. They are puzzle pieces laid in front of me, teaching me a lesson or showing me a path."

"Sounds lame," he said, his lower lip jutted out in a pout.

I chuckled. "It's quite terrifying, still, even after all these years."

In my peripheral, the shimmer of Old Friend's doorknob caught my eye. It was turning, the door creaking open like old joints, and she came hobbling out onto the front porch. Her hair was piled in a candy-floss bun atop her head, held in place by a hair pin that appeared to be some sort of animal bone. Her breasts were swinging, bouncing off her belly with each step. Her knees and hips were out of place, bones stretching flesh, arthritic strain in her movements.

"Old Friend," I greeted.

"Huh?" Aamon said, his eyes following my gaze to the porch of her house.

"Nothing," I said.

"What's that place?" he asked. "It's weird."

I stopped walking. Examined his face, at his eyes that were latched onto Old Friend's house. He saw it, but not her.

"You saw this cabin last night, too," I said. "What do you see?"

Aamon pointed. Right at the little bungalow with the bowl of blood and tears atop the pillars on either side of the deck. Crystals and branches were hanging from the eaves, and the haphazard roof was covered in a blanket of moss. At the little abode that, until now, no one but me could see. Before I had opened Eden's Edge as a campground, I had cordoned off Friend's house so people would leave her space alone.

"What do you see?" I repeated.

"Another cabin, duh," he said.

"Most people can't see it," I said.

"Huh?" he said, brows raised.

Aamon rubbed his eyes. Rubbed again.

"Naw, it's there," he said. "Are the other people blind? Or … I'm a witch!"

And with that, Aamon squealed with glee, dancing about, narrowly avoiding Old Friend who loomed at my side like a bent and withered tree.

"What does this mean?" I whispered to her.

But she wasn't paying attention. She was staring at the road ahead, at the little girl standing there. Half blond hair, half raven black hair, all of her dripping with blood. She was sewn back together with twine the hue of a birch tree, the crude stitching drawing a crooked line from the part of her hair, down the bridge of her nose, and disappearing beneath her pinafore.

"Do you think I can move stuff with my brain, like Carrie from that movie about the prom girl?" Aamon asked as he danced around.

"I don't believe Carrie was a witch," I said. "She was telekinetic."

"But can I do that?" he asked.

"I don't know," I said. "Can you?"

I willed my feet to move, and Old Friend kept pace, her joints popping with each step, a wet and crunchy sound. Aamon followed, his brow furrowing in concentration, his hands thrust forward as if he was trying to move the gravel with the power of his mind. The little girl stood there until we reached her, then she took her place on my other side. Old Friend panted, her white eyes gleaming in the sunlight, her heart pounding so hard I could feel it in my own chest.

"Hello," Aamon said.

As he spoke, the little girl's lips moved too. Her own sound didn't come out, but her lips moved with the words, the voice coming from Aamon himself.

"What's your name?" he asked, her lips forming the words as well.

This time, both their mouths moved with the words, but the sound came from her.

"Lavo," she said.

"Lavo?" he parroted, her lips again moving with his words.

I watched her movements, fluid and soft, her hands curved like a ballerina's in pointe. She was porcelain and unmarked, save the stitching straight down the middle of her, heavily scarred hands, and blackened fingertips. Almost just like me.

"Lavo," she confirmed, enunciating each letter.

Lavo reached her hand out and the boy took it without hesitation. He grimaced and pulled back, but she held tight.

"You're cold," Aamon said. "And squishy."

"I'm dead," Lavo said.

"That's pretty cool," Aamon said.

"Poison," I said.

Lavo nodded. Aamon scrunched his nose.

"That woman talks all confusing," Aamon said to Lavo as he tilted his head at me.

"Your hands and tongue," I said to Lavo. "You dabble in poison."

"That I do," she said, managing to dip into a slight curtsy while continuing to walk forward.

"Lavo," I said. "As in LaVoison."

Lavo beamed. "Yes!"

Aamon huffed. "Tell me!" he said with a whine.

"Catherine Monvoisin, or *LaVosin*," I explained. "A French soothsayer from the 1600s. Dabbled in black magic and poisons. She formed an origination that is believed to be responsible for the death of over two thousand people."

Old Friend growled. I stopped walking.

"Ah," I said, and looked at Lavo. "You are not welcome here."

"I am not a vampire," Lavo said. "I need no invitation."

"You don't belong here," I said.

My knuckles burned with the pressure of my talons beneath. My fear swelled, and with it, my aggression.

"This space is not for you," I said, my voice splitting in two, my bones swelling larger.

"What are you gonna do, Anna," Lavo said. "Burn me? They tried to burn me. You'll see no more success than they did. Besides, maybe you don't belong here. Maybe you'd be better off somewhere else."

"What's going on?" Aamon asked.

He started to shake his arm, trying to free himself of Lavo's grasp, fat tears welling in his eyes.

"I belong here," I said. "This is my home."

"This is your escape," Lavo said. "You settled. You survived. You are hiding, unsure, unhappy. Is that enough?"

My stomach was churning, skin crackling with heat, hearts throbbing in time with Old Friend who was beside me with sharp black teeth sprouting from her empty gums. Everything was about to go to hell in the middle of the day. It hadn't happened since I'd opened Eden as a sanctuary. I had remained in control since the death of Empusa. The monster of me had not been required, wanted, or felt. And now, the heat, the pain, the rage …

"Come now," said Miss Mojo.

Miss Mojo greeted us from down the road. She had come to us in human form, though I could still see her skin crawling with the movement of a myriad of bugs. She belted out a sing-song chuckle that jiggled each and every chin of hers, her black eyes twinkling with daytime stars.

Lavo was gone. Aamon examined his empty hand, which was still grasped around slender fingers that were no longer there.

"Enough foolishness," Lavo scolded. "Let's get on gettin' on and give this baby a show-around."

Aamon scowled, seemingly forgetting his empty grasp.

"I am no baby!" he snapped.

Miss Mojo rested her hands on her shapely hips. "Yes, you is, little man. You's ALL babies to Miss Mojo. Now get your saucy little buns over here and let Miss Mojo teach you a thing or two about this place and its people."

I had intended on showing Aamon around, mostly so I could get to know him better. But Lavo had me more rattled than I'd been in many moons. But now the fog of mystery was clearing, and I could almost put the pieces into place—why Old Friend had returned, why Gus was birthed once more, and why the veil had thinned, allowing the dark unknown to lay slick doubt over my peace. Perhaps nothing was wrong with Eden's Edge.

Maybe I was what was wrong.

Chapter Nine

I pressed my toes into the dirt, kneading the moist soil. Liza was sitting on one of the wide stumps Old Man Merle had hauled into our backyard garden for us to use as seating. After I'd returned home, I'd gone straight to the yard to collect the dead cat and hide it from Liza. Thankfully, Old Man Merle was scooping the last of the intestines out of the grass by the time I got there. Later I would ask him about it.

"I don't know what to make of it," I said. "This Lavo girl."

"Is she like Friend?" Liza asked.

"Not quite?" I said, not really knowing. "Aamon could see her, and I could see her too. He couldn't see Old Friend, though."

I'd told Liza everything about Lavo, including seeing her in the woods the night before we met Ursula and Aamon, and then at the bookstore the day of.

"The appearance of Old Friend is a sure sign something's about to go down," I said.

The last time I saw her, my past had come for me. Mary had tried to get revenge on me for the loss of her childhood.

What was coming this time?

"Do you think it has something to do with Aamon and Ursula?" Liza asked.

"Maybe so," I said. "The timing seems suspicious."

"But you saw her before we even knew about them," Liza said.

"Ursula contacted us with a number she got at an NA meeting, yes?" I said. "So, she knew she was contacting us before we did. Maybe days before she called."

People found out about Eden's Edge through flyers I pinned to walls of old bookshops, witchy boutiques, and occult undergrounds around the province. I advertised us as a kitschy little campground with eccentric owners, accepting of anyone in any condition.

"How would Ursula, in the state she's in, have figured out she could come here and be taken care of? That we wouldn't call the police or Child Welfare Services?"

"Not sure she did," I said. "She may have just been looking for anything. Like my Mom was."

"Is Aamon dangerous?" Liza asked. "I know he's just a boy, but…"

I had been just a girl when Liza watched me tear Bobby limb from limb.

"I will keep a close eye on him," I assured her. "And I'll give Kaz, Miss Mojo, and Merle the rundown, though they're always on alert."

Wings fluttered from above, and a maple leaf fell from the sky.

"Hello, Erinyes," I said.

The headless cardinal landed on my shoulder and nestled against my neck. I gave her a scratch under her belly feathers and her chest gargled with what could have been a song, had she had a neck and a head.

"Come," I said to Erinyes. "I have something for you."

I stood from my stump, but Liza stayed put. I placed my hand on her shoulder and her mouth twitched. She was trying to smile, but there was terror deep within her preventing it.

Could we do it again? Go through another round of violence and horror? And to what end?

I trudged toward the back patio and Liza called after me. "Your feet!"

Ah, yes. My feet were caked in dirt. I was always a mess. I stopped at the side of our cottage and took the hose to rinse my bare feet and calves. When I turned the knob, hot blood flowed from the hose, splashing into the grass and coating my feet with gore. I dropped the hose and Erinyes flapped wildly, her claws piercing both my shirt and shoulder beneath. I called to Liza and she came running.

"What?" she asked.

The blood streaming from the nozzle was filled with globs of fat and shards of bone. The growing puddle of death in the grass caused me to sink. I padded the blood with my foot, splashing red over Liza's legs as well as the side of the cottage.

"Is it cold?" she asked.

Liza bent down, picked up the hose, and dipped her fingers in the thick blood.

Wind rustled through the trees at the back of the yard, sounding like a chorus of furious whispers.

Rancidbitchrancidbitchrancidbitch.

"Nice and cool," Liza said.

I cried when she dipped her lips into the stream from the hose. Blood filled her mouth, and she drank greedily of it, crimson slime coating her golden face and soaking into the black tips of her hair.

"No," I said.

Liza's brow furrowed. The hose began to swell, and the blood stopped streaming. There was a clog beneath the green rubber, swelling, churning. Body parts, bones, flesh, death in some form or another.

I slapped the hose away from Liza's face. She yelped and took a step back. Blood trickled down her chin, but only a small creek of it, birthed from a split on her lower lip.

"What the fuck?" she snapped.

The water at my feet was murky, but from grass and dirt. My legs shimmered with the moisture from clear water. There was no blood other than what I'd drawn.

"You hit me!" Liza said.

"I did," I admitted. "I thought it was blood."

"Thought what was blood?" Liza said.

"The water," I said, holding out the hose.

Liza stared at the crystal stream, then met my gaze. Her eyes were wet, lip swollen.

"I'm sorry," I said.

She said nothing. Her shoulders lifted in a shrug, then she walked away, her eyes on the grass, her fingertips on her wound. The wound I'd inflicted.

Erinyes beat my face with her wing.

"Sorry," I said to her as well.

I stepped to the side, out of the mud puddle I'd created, and properly cleaned the dirt off my feet. Once I was satisfied I'd track minimal mess through the cabin, I closed the faucet and went inside. Once we were in the bedroom, I pressed my finger against Erinyes's belly to get her to perch there, then I set her on the dresser in front of the squirrel parts.

"Gus is back," I told her.

In response, Gus stood, shaking and stretching as Erinyes went wild fluttering over him and embracing him with her wings. I let them reconnect, and I sat on the bed, enjoying the quiet and the solitude. That solace didn't last for long. An infant's wail shrieked from outside, so sharp and loud that it startled the grey jays out of the trees. I leapt to the window and looked outside, but there was nothing I could see. There was no activity around the four cabins; Ursula was asleep in her cabin, And Kaz was rocking in the chair on her porch. Marie was out picking vegetables from her garden, and Mojo and Merle were having a great yarn by the fire pit. And there weren't any tents or any vehicles, and no one was expected for another week.

The infant wailed again. The sound was coming from everywhere, both far and near. I walked down the hall, toward the front door, but stopped at Mary's room to look inside.

Mary was sitting on the floor with two tow-headed children, playing with a wooden train set. Her smile was so big, and her laughter loud as they played and chatted. Her legs were plump and pink as she got up and chased the children around the room, tossing a pillow at the eldest to make her laugh.

They all stopped suddenly, and their head spun toward me.

"You took this from me," Mary said. She was an adult, but the voice was that of a child. Of the playful child I knew before she'd been broken. She screamed, and the noise consumed me. "You ruin everything! Fucking halfbreed tainted bitch!"

Mary and the children lunged for me. I couldn't react in time before their fingernails found my flesh, their teeth tearing away strips of meat until my bones were exposed.

Another wail. These children were too old for a baby's cry. The sound knocked me out of my vision, and there was Mary, grey and fragile, propped up in her bed. Her eyes were fixed on me in a glare of rage. She couldn't move on her own, couldn't speak. Couldn't live.

What kind of life is this?

"Liza will get your chair," I said. My whole body was trembling. "Take you outside. I'll call for her …"

The wail intensified. It was coming from the front yard. I ran out the front door and my breasts exploded with waves of pain. I cupped them and found them engorged and rock hard. Milk poured from my nipples, soaking through my bra and shirt. I brought the fabric of my clothing to my mouth and sucked. The milk was sour. Its stench was so bad and tasted so foul, I vomited over myself in violent heaves. The baby wailed, and I ripped off my shirt and bra, dropping them on my doorstep as I ran toward the woods.

Branches clawed at my body as I sprinted through the trees, milk leaking from my nipples and blood pouring from my vagina. I shed all my clothes, which made the cut of the thorns worse, but I didn't slow down until I reached the cemetery.

The wailing had crescendoed to a deafening scream, pain-filled and mournful. Old Man Merle stood in the center of the cemetery, his body convulsing and his arms flailing above his head.

"Merle?"

His head snapped toward me, and once he was facing me, I realized that shrill cry was coming from him.

"Gahhhh!" he shrieked and flapped his arms at the lychgate.

"Merle, what's …"

I saw, and a scream built in my belly. Creatures were squeezing through the lychgate, the air parting and stretching like a vagina. What slithered out wasn't human, or animal, or any kind of beast I'd ever seen. Each creature had too many legs, not enough eyes, so many teeth. Scales, bones, feathers, and decaying meat. Small, large, all either eating each other or fucking each other's faces, asses, or open wounds. The cemetery soaked up the steaming black blood that gushed from this rift, and Merle started sinking into the softening ground.

"Merle!" I screeched.

He was already reaching for me as I contorted and changed. My talons emerged, my limbs elongated, and my body became a mass of bone and dirt. Merle tried to hug me, hold me back, but I swiped him to the side. One by one I grabbed these creatures and ripped them to shreds, consuming them as I went until my belly stretched and tightened, and bloat pained my chest. Even then, I kept going, the waste of these creatures leaking out of my anus and soaking into the ground along with the blood.

But they kept coming. I bellowed and rammed the lychgate with my body. The whole thing listed to the side, leaning into the rift until the fog tightened and it pinched closed.

I fell to the ground, my body retracting into itself. Old Man Merle crumpled beside me and scooped me up in his arms. We rocked, I breathed, Merle gahhhh'd, and the sounds and feel of normal night resumed.

"What's happening?" I asked Merle.

"Gahhhh," he moaned, and ran his bony, necrotic fingers through my hair.

It was the same as when I was a child, with Old Man Merle as my protector and me as his only friend. And here we were, where we first met, entwined in the cemetery in the fucking dirt.

Beside us was a freshly dug grave. Merle didn't do that. I know he didn't. But it was there, and I knew it was meant for me. I leaned over and peeked inside. Lavo was laid out in the dirt, her dress crisp and clean, her white hair curled into ringlets and her black hair shiny and smooth. Her lips were painted a glossy red, and the large scar down the middle of her was the colour of starlight. She was so, so pretty and peaceful that I almost crawled down to be with her. When I leaned over further, readying myself to fall in, Lavo split in two. One side of her, the ringlet side, was filled with blood that soaked into the dirt. The other side was filled with a sparkling clear fluid that sloshed out of that half of the body into the earth below. I knew if I tasted it, I'd taste tears. Possibly my own.

"I can't do this, Merle," I said. "I just want quiet and normal."

"Gahhhh."

Chapter Ten

I woke up with dirt in my mouth. Merle was gone, and my head rested on a toppled headstone. My body was caked in milk, blood, and gore. My bones ached, and I stretched like Gus, popping joints and warming muscles. I rolled up onto my knees, braced myself against the headstone, and stood.

Dawn was breaking, its pink and purple fingers reaching through the morning mist. Old Friend stood in front of the tilted lychgate. She was crooked and grey, her silhouette rocking from foot to foot, fluid drip, drip, dripping from all the holes in her body.

"Old Friend," I said.

We stood together, hand in hand, looking through the opening of the lychgate.

"The world thins here," I said.

Old Friend was a stoic woman. She looked like she'd weathered many storms. I wondered what she'd been through in our years apart. I'd spent a short period of time with her as a child, then another brief period in my thirties, and now …

How long did we have together? How long would each of us live? What would become of her once I was gone?

"How long do we have?" I asked her. "This time. Together."

She didn't answer. She looked so old.

"Is this the last time we'll see each other?"

I didn't know this woman, but she was me. And I was fading fast. All the years I had been avoiding myself, denying myself, running, hiding. I'd wasted a lifetime. And now hell had come for me. Was I the one tearing the veil? An angry spirit trying to decide her place?

Liza was in danger. Everyone was. I knew it in my bones.

Old Friend tugged my arm. I followed as she led me away from the cemetery, back down the forest path toward Eden's Edge. Dead things lined the trail—birds, rodents, deer. The forest floor was covered in tentacles of rot, thinning the further we got from the cemetery.

"We haven't much time," I said.

I didn't know what I meant by that, but it's what I felt.

Back in Eden's Edge, the dawn had glowed up from pink to orange, the flowers opening and the birds singing. I strained against Old Friend, pulling toward my home, but she held tight and pulled me toward hers. When we got there, up those steps and between the bowls of blood and tears, she released my hand.

"Okay," I said. "Thanks for walking me back."

She would go inside, and I would watch the door close. I'd hear locks engage and the creak of her footsteps on the old wooden floors inside. I'd go my merry way, back home, and cuddle in with Liza and continue my routine, day after day, and deal with things as they attacked.

But that's not what happened. Old Friend wrapped her long fingers around the red knob and turned it, then leaned her shoulder into the door and opened it wide.

I wanted to peek inside. I'd never, in all these years, seen the inside of Old Friend's house.

Turns out I didn't have to peek. She walked inside, disappeared into the dark, and left the door wide open.

My flesh crackled with lightning as I stepped over the threshold. Once I was inside, the door slammed shut behind me. I screamed and fumbled for a knob. There was no knob. I couldn't see a thing in the dark. The windows must have been covered, and the lights were off. Or perhaps there were no lights at all.

"I can't see," I whimpered, hoping Old Friend would take pity on me.

A faint glow flickered into the corner, multiplying into two, three, four, as candles sparked to life around the room. Within a couple of breaths, the room was illuminated by dozens of dancing flames that threw impossible shadows on the walls. Shadows that looked like moose, birds, bears, wolves, trees, rocks. Buildings and cars. Drinks and jewels. But the room itself was empty and large. As large as the cabin and then some. There were no other rooms, just the single, big open space. No pictures on the walls, no decorations, no furniture, save one piece. A chesterfield against the far wall.

Three people were sitting on the chesterfield, still as statues. New Friend on the left, Friend in the center, and Old Friend on the right. New Friend was in her jumper and black patent shoes, blood around her collar and no head attached to her neck. Friend was all limbs, teeth, and black eyes, her joints and bones contorted every which way. And Old Friend was grey and withered, breasts puddled on her thighs, white sprouts of hair dotting her scalp and labia.

"Friends?" I said.

The flames of the candles trembled when I spoke, and the shadows formed into many Friends. New Friends milling about—little girls, none with heads, all wearing different out-fits. There were many Friends, too, some with hooves, others with wings, all with long black hair, too many teeth, and empty eyes. And Old Friends toddled around with canes and walkers, holding their backs, skin pocked with age spots, stretch marks, and scars.

"Who are you?" I asked. "What are you?"

All their jaws moved in unison, and the New Friends' heads bobbed in time with their words.

Fog and steam,
Gossamer and pitch,
Halfbreed tainted rotten bitch.

Their voices filled my head. All the sounds, scents, and sights of the world filled me. Lives I'd never known, people I could have been. I cried, screamed, and The Friends got louder—reminders of what I was, what I was not, and what I could have been.

"Stop!" I screamed, and still they made noise, all of them on their feet now, dancing and twirling around the room to the crackling of an old turntable in some faraway place.

I was swept up in the sea of Friends, and we danced, their hands fondling me, their eyes in my sockets, their tongues in my mouth. I tasted a million different foods, pul-sated with a million pleasures, reeled from endless pain.

"Let me go!"

They all stopped moving and faced me. The ones who had heads opened their mouths, and the sound of a baby's wailing blasted out of every mouth. I screamed, dropped to my knees, covered my ears, and they bawled louder. The noise made my eyeballs throb, and my nipples began drib-bling milk again. I crawled to the door and clawed the wood until splinters pierced beneath my nails, peeling them off. I clawed and scratched until the tips of my fingers ripped away and bone poked through.

There was a knock at the door and the beating of wings.

The Friends scattered like roaches, leaving only one Friend in the living room. Old Friend. She sauntered to the door, sniffling and simpering a baby's woes, and rested her hand on the wood.

"Open it," I said.

She did not open it.

"Open it, you cunt!" I screamed.

Whatever was on the other side of the door started howling and beating on the wood. Old Friend covered her ears and scampered away into the shadows.

The wood splintered and a bloody fist appeared through the gash. The fingers uncurled, grasped the wood, and ripped the door apart. Once the space was big enough, I squeezed through, tearing the skin on my ribs and outer thighs in the process.

"Merle," I gasped.

Old Man Merle was angry. His brow was furrowed together in a single, angry caterpillar and his fists balled as he squinted into the dark cabin.

"GAHHHH!" he bellowed. A threat.

Erinyes was there, too, beating her wings against the outside walls. She fluttered to the bowl of tears and submerged herself, shaking droplets like crystals off her feathers. I followed her lead, scooping the liquid and washing myself as best I could. I was still naked, and there was milk and blood smeared all over my body.

Merle lifted his foot with the yellow boot on and tried to take a step in the door, but Old Friend lunged out of the darkness and slammed another door in the old one's place.

"Gahhhh," Merle grumbled.

"Yeah," I said. "A right twat."

Merle's brow relaxed as he turned his attention from the door to me. He scooped water on my body to cleanse the tears from the splintered door that ran up my sides like I'd been swiped by a dragon.

"It's okay, Merle," I lied.

Tears were pouring from Merle's eyes as he gently washed away debris and blood, taking care not to touch my more delicate areas. He was always the gentleman. He grunted and struggled down to one knee, where he began washing my feet, then paused when something caught his eye.

I saw it, too. Tendrils of black rot like the stuff from the cemetery. It was stuck to the bottom of his single boot and squished up between the toes on his barefoot. He rocked back on his haunches and started scrubbing it away.

My eyes followed the trail of black pitch from Old Friend's door, down her steps, and into the grass where we'd walked. Old Friend and I had dragged this back here on our feet.

"Here," I said to Merle. "Let me help."

I tried. But no matter how hard we both scrubbed, Merle's boot and foot would not come clean. Nor my feet, or the porch.

"The land is spoiling," I said. "It will spread."

Merle looked up at me, face wide and strained with despair.

"I'll stop it," I assured him. "I'll figure it out. It's just something seeping through. Demonic, likely."

I scanned the high tree branches for signs of Khuya—my father. Whenever fuckery was afoot, he was typically close behind. But there was nothing lurking there this night. Not that I could see. Merle had started picking at Old Friend's porch in a futile attempt to clean off the vines of rot, and Erinyes perched back on my shoulder, her nails poking into my skin.

My friends. My family. The only people I had. All of them, right here in this campground. Old Man Merle, Gus, Erinyes, Miss Mojo, Mary. Liza, who meant more than life or death to me. And they were all in danger.

"I have to go," I said to Merle, covering my mouth with my hand so he didn't see the beginnings of sobs.

He paid no mind as I hurried down the steps and ran across the grass, aiming for my home, my mind and hearts beating and churning, overwhelmed and frantic.

Chapter Eleven

Liza held a cup of tea out in front of me. I slithered my hands out of the cocoon of a crocheted blanket she'd wrapped me in when I first burst through the door and grasped the tea for warmth and comfort. Ursula hadn't been there, thank goodness; I had been shivering and pert near blue from the crisp night air.

"Thank you," I said.

The mug was hot. I spread my hands wide and pressed as much skin as I could against the ceramic to warm myself.

"Will that heal?" Liza asked, her eyes on my hands.

My fingertips were gone, shredded away, bone poking through.

I shrugged. Typically, I went right back to normal after my body had shifted to its demonic form. These weren't demon hands, though. They were mine, my human hands, and I cringed at the thought that I might have destroyed them. What had been a mild case of rot was now bare-bone fingertips and capillaries of black pitch. How long before I was more death than life? I shifted my weight from one leg to the other, quietly assessing the wounds on my sides. I hoped they weren't seeping into the blanket. Liza had spent nearly half a year crocheting it.

"I went inside Old Friend's house," I said.

Liza sat beside me on the couch; her hands wrapped around her own mug of tea.

"I thought you couldn't go in there," she said.

"I never could," I said. "But she left the door open for me this time."

"What was inside?" Liza asked.

"Friends," I said. "Lots of them. The little headless girl, the arachnid woman, the old hag. The ones *I* knew were sitting on the couch. But there were lots of others. Different versions of the originals."

"What do you make of it?" she asked.

"I think they were possibilities," I said. "Iterations of me that would have been something else had I made different choices, been given different paths."

I thought of the shoes that made up the base of New Friend's house the first time I knew her. All different dress shoes, cheap and expensive, worn and shiny, with all manner of dead feet inside. All the children I could have been. All the shoes that could have carried me forward in a million different directions.

"What was she showing you?" Liza asked.

"What I could have been?" I said. "Different outcomes?"

"But …" Liza pressed her teeth into her lower lip, like she always did when she was worried. Or sad.

I said it for her. "It's too late," I said. "It was cruel of her. I don't want to think what could have been. What I've lost, what I never had."

A childhood, a career, peace, normalcy.

Liza put her tea on the table.

"I love you," she said.

She took my face in her hands and kissed me, pressing her lips firmly against mine.

"I love you," she said again when she pulled away. "You've been through so much."

"*We've* been through so much," I said.

"And we're still standing," she said. "I regret the years we didn't have, but we're here now."

"We could have gone to school together," I said. "Gone to school at *all*. Had careers, traveled the world …"

Liza took my tea from me, set it on the table, and grasped my hands firm enough for them to ache.

"We are not dead," she said, looking deep and hard into my eyes. "We still have life to live and we're going to live it."

"We don't have much time," I said.

"We aren't even fifty," she said.

"Just about," I said, "but that's not what I meant. At the cemetery, the lychgate, there's something growing there. Seeping through, spoiling the land, and—"

"Not now," Liza said. "You don't have to fix everything. Just let it be for now and let's live."

"But if I can stop it—" I said.

"And if you can't?"

If I couldn't …

Hell, I didn't even know what the rot was. I assumed that shit was leaking through from a nastier side of the veil, but why? And what was it going to do? The creatures coming through … were they real, or flecks in my perception? Aamon hadn't been there watching me shower, and I didn't give birth to a human baby. Maybe there was nothing in the cemetery after all. Maybe no creatures were coming to devour anything and everything I loved.

"Anna," Liza said, putting her hands on my shoulders. "I can see your mind racing. Slow down and join me here, in this moment, right here in this place."

When Liza leaned in to kiss me, I kissed back, concentrating on the softness of her lips, of the smell of the pine trees clinging to her hair. I took her face in my hands and parted her lips with my tongue, breathing in her breath and tasting the sweet flowers of the tea in her mouth. I shrugged the blanket off my shoulders, and cold air found my nipples, drawing them erect. Liza kissed my chin, and I tilted my head back, giving her access to my throat. She dragged her tongue in a wavy line down my neck, between my breasts, then curved to the side to take my nipple in her mouth.

I laid back on the couch and the blanket fell open, exposing me. Liza moved with me, latched onto my nipple where she circled her tongue and sucked, gently nipping with her teeth. Her hand moved up my thigh, kneading the flesh there, fingers walking like a spider until she parted me. Wetness coated her fingers as she placed her thumb on my clit, three fingers in my vagina, and her pinky in my ass. She massaged into me in slow, firm thrusts, rubbing her own sex against my knee as she moved inside me. I came, the pulsing of my muscles nearly pushing her hand out of me, my juices gushing onto the chesterfield.

Instead of feeling relief, though, I felt a need so intense I didn't know what to do with it. I sat up with her hand still inside me, forcing it deep so I tore slightly before she could pull it out. I pulled her to her feet and lifted her shirt over her head as she shimmied out of her pants. We were animals, naked and groping each other, and when she brushed against my clit, I held her in place and climaxed against her, surprised at the ease with which the second wave came.

I sat her down on the coffee table and spread her legs, eating her, rolling and flicking my tongue until she was humping my face and gushing down my chin. And we still frantically fondled other, fitting ourselves together like a puzzle, our labia rubbing together and our nipples brushing as we ground together, pushing hard, clits throbbing together until we climaxed. It was violent and messy, fluid squirting everywhere, Liza screaming and pulsating so heavy I could feel the muscles of her labia contracting against mine. I pulsed with pleasure from my clit to my rectum as I released, and all of me seemed to gush into Liza, and her into me.

We shifted over to the couch, our limbs tangled, sweat and release making our bodies slide against each other. I grabbed the blanket and covered us, me on top of Liza, her legs wrapped around me, bodies pressed together. I rested my head on her breasts and listened to the beating of her heart. It slowed, as did her breathing, and soon, she was sound asleep beneath me. My eyes fluttered, slumber slowly winning out, but I was jolted back to consciousness by a sound. A baby crying.

No, there was nothing. I focused on the sound, but it was gone.

My eyes fluttered again, and black tendrils seeped in through the windows. They reached for me like hands, many arms clawing in all directions. I followed a particularly elongated hand as it coiled toward the hall, and the figure standing there.

Mary was there. Had she been watching us? She was naked, her scarred and crooked body pale in the dark hallway. She was fingering herself and crying. Yes. She'd been watching us, and she was both aroused and angry by what we had, about what she'd never had.

The hand reached her, brushing its fingers up her chest, then wrapping its two-long fingers around her throat. A hiss of air escaped her as the hands lifted her into the air until the wisps of blonde hair atop her head touched the ceiling. There she hung, feet dangling and arms limp at her sides as her lips faded from white, to purple, to blue, then finally black. Her bladder and bowels released with a splash on the floor as life finally left her body.

"No," I whispered.

Erinyes flew into the room and circled Mary, the flapping of her wings dissipating the image like fog. Mary wasn't there, nor were the hands. The walls and windows were bare, too. I assessed the rest of the room, and found that the black tendrils were gone, if they'd ever been there at all.

When sleep finally took me, there was nothing but faint crying in some other somewhere, and shadows of black rot in my mind.

Chapter Twelve

When I awoke, I was still on top of Liza, her legs around me but lolled to the side. Her face was strained; even in sleep, her eyes twitching beneath closed lids. So much past trauma, and now whatever this mess was. Would she have been better off without me?

No. Allison and Bobby would have killed her.

But after she got away from them, maybe she should have gotten away from me, too.

I peeled my body off Liza's and rolled off the couch. Once on my feet, I covered her with the blanket and tiptoed away. For once I'd be the one to make her coffee and breakfast. The sun wasn't up yet, but the sky was lightening. I wanted to check in on Ursula and Aamon, and touch base with Marie about the upcoming camping reservations. I'd eventually have to make my way back to the cemetery and see about that mess, but for now, I was going to do what Liza said and live in the moment.

Once the coffee was on, I had a quick shower, dressed,

and wandered outside. Erinyes and Gus were waiting for me, scrapping and chittering up in the eaves of the house. Gus was a lot louder now since he was all bones from his neck to his missing tail, no fur to soften his movements; his ribs scratched along the shingles as he tore around, hopping and jumping at Erinyes who flapped and dove at him from above.

"Knock it off," I scolded them. "Liza's sleeping."

Like petulant children, they didn't knock it off entirely, but at least they moved their ruckus to the grass where they wouldn't be so loud. They followed along beside me as I walked down the lane to cabin four where hopefully Ursula and Aamon were resting peacefully.

"Mornin,' sunshine!" Miss Mojo said as I approached the porch of cabin four. "You're up awful early. Or late?"

Miss Mojo hadn't changed a bit since I'd met her. A large woman, both in stature and personality, she took up space and filled hearts wherever she went. She'd saved me more than once and had been a solid mentor in the ways of witchcraft and the world. She was sitting on the porch, rocking in a chair Old Man Merle had made out of elk antlers and two by fours.

"Early, actually," I said. "I slept, for a change."

A grin squished Miss Mojo's cheeks up, squeezing her deep brown eyes to slits. "You done more than just snooze, methinks. I smell pleasure on you."

I smiled, and a small throb radiated between my legs, a memory of the explosive releases the night before.

"They good?" I said, nodding to the cabin that contained Ursula and Aamon.

"She's a mess," Miss Mojo said, "but that's to be expected. I wouldn't let her shoot none of that poison into herself yesterday. She gotta suffer a touch to get through, but she'll make it. She was all shakes and pukes until I knocked her out with some kava and Valerian root."

"Is that safe mixed together?" I asked.

Miss Mojo shrugged. "Safer than heroin. I gave her a hefty dose and kept checking her through the night. No small task, I'll tell you, and not cuz of her. That youngin of hers is *off*."

"Off?" I said.

"Yessum," Miss Mojo said. "He looked right tuckered last night, so I scooted his ass to bed. He stayed right there, but I can't be sure he slept. He sat up on his bed all night, eyes dead and staring at something I couldn't see."

"He was awake?" I asked.

"Dunno," she said. "Didn't move, not even blink. And he answered none of my questions. I even spat some bees at him, but he didn't flinch."

Miss Mojo had command of all the insects, and conjured ones she needed. Came in handy more than once. Now that she was dead, she seemed to have an even bigger arsenal of creepy crawlies.

"Speaking of bugs," I said. "I found some odd beetles the other night."

"Where at?" she asked.

"The woods," I said.

"Ain't nothin' odd about beetles in the woods, girl," she chuckled.

"I've never seen ones like these before," I said. "They were big and mottled all calico."

"Were they in the trees?" she asked. "Or munching on a carcass?"

"Kind of munching, I suppose …" I said.

Miss Mojo scrunched her face at me. Her plump red lips looked like a closed rose bloom.

"You seeing things?" she asked.

"Always," I said.

"New things?" she clarified, arms crossed over the shelf of her breasts.

"Yeah," I said. "And Old Friend is back. And Gus."

"Fuck, help us," Miss Mojo said, making symbols with her hands and chanting something beneath her breath.

"I know," I said. And there's some sort of rot spreading out at the cemetery. Things coming through the lychgate, too."

Miss Mojo stood and thumped her hands onto her hips. "None of this is small news, Miss Anna. You shoulda come to me sooner so we could get this sorted."

"I know, I know," I said. "Let's start with the bugs and go from there."

"Why do you think the bugs have anything to do with any of it?" she asked.

"Because they came out of a little girl I saw in the woods," I said. "They were inside her when I ripped her in half."

"Huh," Miss Mojo said. "Human child? Former or otherwise?"

I shook my head. "I don't think."

"Yes, that does sound mighty suspicious," she said. "Have you seen this girl before or since?"

"Not before," I said, "but after, in Chapters, right before we went to meet Ursula and Aamon at the diner."

"Trouble," Miss Mojo mumbled as she looked over at the door of cabin four. "Your little girl, this momma and her spawn. Ain't none of this feels very good."

It didn't. And in my experience, visions like this didn't accompany pleasant changes in my life.

"Well, lemme see these bugs then," Miss Mojo said.

"They're in a jar buried in my garden," I said. "Beside the daffodils. I marked the top with a yellow rock."

Miss Mojo nodded.

"Miss Liza won't notice the dirt moving about back there, if I start rooting around?" Miss Mojo asked.

"She's seen worse, and she's aware of you," I said. "Besides, I think she may actually sleep in for a change."

Miss Mojo smiled wide and large, then yanked me in for a hug and patted me on the back.

"Atta girl," she said. "You done good pleasin' your woman."

And with that, Miss Mojo let out a jolly chuckle and waddled toward my house.

I wished I could be that jovial, especially in light of the forthcoming task. I knocked gently, then with more force before entering cabin four. The living room was clean, mostly due to the fact that Ursula and Aamon had arrived at Eden's Edge with next to nothing. The kitchen was a little more haphazard. A couple of plates were strewn about, food on the coffee table, and a bag of milk left out on the counter. I laid my hand on it. Still cool, so not spoiled yet. I put the bag in the fridge and made a mental note to stock a few more groceries. Ursula might not have much of an appetite yet, but Aamon was a growing boy. Or … whatever he was. And boys, or whatevers, tended to lean toward ravenous at all times.

I checked on Ursula first. As reported by Miss Mojo, Ursula was dead to the world. She was on her back, snoring at the ceiling, her body a fit of twitches and shivers. I got another blanket from her closet to cover her up, then turned her onto her side. She responded to my touch, leaning in and smiling before curling herself tight into the fetal position.

Next stop, Aamon's room. Also as reported, Aamon was sitting on the edge of his bed, feet resting on the floor and hands set on his thighs, eyes fixed on the wall.

"You like the wallpaper?" I asked.

No answer.

I sat next to him. We sat like that for a spell. I let silence hang heavy in the room, hoping the discomfort of that would prompt him to move or say something. Eventually, he did. He stood and walked toward the wall without acknowledging I was in the room. He got to it, then traced a finger in a repeating pattern over the wallpaper. Words? I couldn't tell. I tried to make out the shapes but just couldn't.

Aamon stopped touching the wall, turned abruptly, and left the room. I followed him across the hall to Ursula's room.

"Oh," I gasped.

Ursula was on the floor, blood pouring from her arm and soaking her nightgown with the blanket puddled around her. The opposite hand held a swiss army knife which shook and rattled in her trembling grasp. I dropped to my knees beside her and examined her arm. Her left arm was cut open from wrist to the crook of her elbow. And deep, too, almost a centimeter from the look of it, though it was hard to tell with the blood pouring out.

"Aamon, honey, could you …"

No, he could not. His face was blank, his eyes distant. He was looking at his mother, but it didn't seem like he was really seeing her. I got to my feet and sprinted to the bathroom. I grabbed some antiseptic, then thought better of it. This wound needed more than sterilization. Ursula needed medical attention. I texted Liza and got to work. I had to staunch the flow so Ursula wouldn't bleed out before we got her into town. I grabbed a towel from under the sink and ran to the kitchen to grab some shears. I was already cutting the towel into strips as I went back to the room.

When I got there, Aamon was gone, and Ursula was laying down in a puddle of her own blood.

"Good," I said. "Better to have you all the way down before you pass out and hit your head."

I tied a tourniquet above Ursula's elbow, and a second one for good measure, then wrapped the remainder of the towel around the wound and wrapped it tight with duct tape. Once she was all bandaged up, I moved her away from the blood puddle and cleaned her up as best I could, including slipping off her nightgown and dressing her in sweatpants and a t-shirt.

Once that was all done, all that was left to do before Liza

arrived was to get Aamon ready to go. I went back across to his room to retrieve him and found him standing in front of the wall again.

"Aamon, I am going to take your mom to the hospital," I said. "You can come, or you can stay here with Miss …"

The wallpaper, which was a soft yellow decorated with silver flowers, was now smeared in wet crimson. Aamon turned his body to me, almost as if he was showing off the front of his jammies, which were soaked with blood. His face, too, and his hands. On the wall he had finger-painted an image. Three hearts squished together.

"Aamon," I breathed. "How…"

Aamon pointed at my chest, at the three hearts that beat there, then turned back to the wallpaper and started clawing at it. The paper peeled away until the drawing of the heart was in his hands. He turned to me once more. I reached out for the image of the hearts, but he did not hand it to me. He tore off a strip, balled it up, tossed it in his mouth, then swallowed it with a strained, dry gulp. Then another strip, and another, until the heart was all gone.

"Anna."

"Liza," I answered.

She was standing in Aamon's doorway, staring at him.

"Why is he bloody?" she asked. "Is he hurt, too?"

"No," I said. "The blood is his mother's."

"Why is he …" Liza hesitated, looked at the wall. "What did he …"

"Later," I said. "Let's get Ursula in the car. I was going to leave Aamon with Marie, but he needs to stay close to me."

Liza asked no further questions.

"Come," I said to Aamon.

I placed my hand on the small of his back and guided him out of the room. Liza went across the hall and got Ursula to her feet, and the two of them stumbled out of the bloody carnage of cabin four. As we got into the car, which Liza had driven across the campsite right up to the front porch, I motioned to a swarm of bees nearby. They buzzed in a flurry, then shot off into the woods to go fetch Old Man Merle. Merle and Miss Mojo would have cabin four all cleaned up by the time we returned, with or without Ursula and Aamon in tow.

Chapter Thirteen

I hated hospitals. I had no experience with them in childhood, and in adulthood, I'd avoided them at all costs. I'd never really needed one myself, on account of my biology being magic and cursed all at once. And the times I did end up in one, I was interrogated by a cop who turned out to be a vengeful demon. Good times.

Now, I had to explain Ursula's situation to a doctor, which was a violation and betrayal, so I didn't.

"This is not my story to tell," I explained to the doctor.

"Okaaay," he said, really slow as he looked at his chart and not at me. "I do need some history, please."

"I have limited history for her," I said. "Her name is Ursula, and she and her son are staying at my … place."

The doctor looked at Ursula, who was sleeping soundly in her hospital bed thanks to a cocktail of painkillers and sedatives.

"Your place," he said.

"Yes," I said. "My place."

"A house?" he asked. "Or …"

"Or" I answered.

I said no more. In case this wasn't a good idea, and we needed to get out, he couldn't know where to find us.

The doctor picked up Ursula's good arm and rolled it to the side, exposing the bruises of track marks.

"What was her condition when she arrived at your *place*?" he asked.

I sighed. "Like you'd imagine," I said. "Withdrawals; sickly. I gave her and her son a place to stay."

"You didn't think to call the authorities?" he asked, now making eye contact with me.

"I help people," I said. "I've often given space to people who aren't in a good situation."

"She has a child with her," he said, "whose welfare you didn't question?"

"Aamon is safe," I said.

"And who will tend to him while she's here?" the doctor asked.

"How long will you keep her?" I asked.

The doctor sighed and took off his glasses. "Here in British Columbia, we can institute a forty-eight-hour involuntary hold. During that hold, a psychiatrist will assess her, and will either determine she's fit to leave, or will complete Form 4.2 to hold her for a month, which I imagine is what they'll do."

"I only wanted you to tend to her arm," I said.

"Which we did," he said. "She's all stitched up and full of antibiotics. But who's to say she won't open herself back up?"

"I'll provide better supervision," I said.

"Is that really your place?" he argued. "This is an odd task for someone like you to take on."

"Someone like me?" I said. The tone that came out of

me was more combative than I intended. Definitely more defensive. "I am capable—"

"I'm not suggesting you're not capable," the doctor said with his palm raised to pacify me, "but I do question why you'd want the responsibility."

"Sometimes I help people," I repeated. "I've taken in abused women, homeless people, addicts. I lived on the street once. I know … it's not easy. All she wanted was some safety for her and her son. I gave her that and can continue to provide that until she's ready to get help."

The doctor sighed and jotted down something in his charts.

"I admire your generosity, weird as it is, but sometimes help must be forced upon people," he said. "She needs treatment, both for the drugs and the suicidal ideation. And legal process must be followed to ensure the boy's care."

"But—"

"That's my final word on it," the doctor said as he shut his chart. "Ursula will be staying for forty-eight hours, and Child and Family Services will be coming for the child. They aren't going to take him from her, but he needs to be placed somewhere safe while his mother gets healthy again."

"But—"

The doctor stood and loomed over me. "You are not next of kin. You don't know where they came from, what their medical histories are, and you don't have the education, experience, or authority to care for them. End of story."

And with that, he strode out of the room, the stomping of his feet punctuating his final word on the matter.

The doctor wasn't wrong. I knew that. Ursula was in great danger of injuring or killing herself and needed medical intervention where the addiction was concerned. And Aamon needed to be somewhere safe, though I wasn't sure a foster home or temporary care facility was quite the right place for him.

Selfishly, I needed them back at Eden's Edge where I could keep an eye on them. They didn't come into my life for no reason. They came on the heels of Old Friend and Lavo and had brought Gus and the rot of hell with them. Aamon was more than a little boy and had secrets of vital importance locked within him.

No, they could not be taken from me.

"What's the story?" Liza asked.

She slipped into the room, Aamon's hand held in hers. She let him go and he climbed into the chair at Ursula's bedside, put his head on her belly, and gazed up at her face.

"They want to keep her," I said.

"For how long?" Liza asked.

"Forty-eight-hour hold," I said. "Then at least a month. Psych involuntary order."

Liza nodded. "Yeah. Sounds like that's for the best."

"It isn't," I bit back. "They need to come back to Eden's Edge."

"Anna," Liza said. "Ursula is sick. And we have no experience caring for children."

"Miss Mojo can help us," I said. "She was a teacher. And we'll keep a better eye on Ursula. We can help her—"

"Why?" Liza asked. "It isn't safe, Anna. Not for her, maybe not for us. Why would we do this when she has options? She's here now, at the hospital, and someone will take care of Aamon until she can."

"No!" I bellowed.

When I yelled, it came out as three voices layered on top of each other. My teeth elongated in my mouth and my eyes widened, causing the room to pulse red in my vision and spike in clarity. The colour drained from Liza's face and her lip began to tremble.

I took a breath, willed my temperature to lower, and softened my tone.

"There's something about them," I explained, slow and

quiet. "They came to Eden's Edge for a reason, and all the abnormal things accompanying them? They are heralding something I need to deal with."

An itch tingled at the hairline on the back of my head. I dug my nails in to scratch it, and the sensation of a myriad of spider's feet tingled over my neck. I wiped and scratched, and bloody black rot sloughed off under my nails.

"Are you okay?" Liza asked.

But she took a step back instead of coming to me.

"Fine," I said. "Just this damn rash."

Liza's mouth was a tight line. She looked over at Aamon and Ursula, then at the floor.

"Do what you need to do," she said.

"Can you bring the car around?" I asked. "But to the back parkade. We'll come out the rear entrance, past the imaging department."

"Sure," Liza said. "Come, Aamon. Let's go get the car."

Aamon did as he was told. Liza took his hand but continued looking at the floor as she slunk out of the room, leading Aamon along beside her. Guilt was a boulder in my chest, cutting off my air, but there was also fear. Fear of Ursula and Aamon, fear of what plagued me and Eden's Edge, and fear of losing Liza. I looked at Ursula splayed out on the bed and hesitated.

I could leave her there and let the hospital take care of her. I could allow them to put Aamon into foster care, where they would be better equipped to tend to his needs. I could focus on Liza, on Eden's Edge, and not get involved with business that might or might not have anything to do with me.

From behind me, a growl.

The bathroom door was slightly ajar, but not enough to allow light to illuminate what was inside.

"Hello?" I said.

Old Friend hissed. She was sitting in the chair in the corner of the hospital room, gums bared, growling at the open bathroom door.

Oh.

"Khuya," I said to my father, who I was certain lurked behind that door.

The door squealed as it opened wider, revealing the looming dark demon within. He was as tall as the ceiling and then some, having to hunch to clear the door frame as he stepped out into the hospital room. His four cocks were flaccid, swinging around his tree-trunk thighs like a meaty hula skirt. He used to fluff them erect to make me uncomfortable, but now that the shock of them had worn off, he didn't bother.

The stench radiating off him was pert near unbearable. Spoiled meat and fresh-dead skunk, with the tang of hot semen. This was not a new odour from him, but sour enough that it caused me to recoil. No one could ever get used to that reek.

I didn't ask why he had appeared. He came, just like Old Friend had come. They each took a side of Ursula's bed, slid their hands and talons beneath her arms, and lifted her into the air. If anyone walked in at that moment, they would see Ursula hanging from nothing, arms extended as in crucifixion, head lolled to the side like death. They floated Ursula toward me until she was in front of me, then lowered her until her feet touched the ground.

"Time to go," I said to her, my mind made up by Old Friend and Khuya. Witch and Demon.

I bore Ursula's weight, which nearly toppled me to the ground.

"I can't walk out with her like this," I said.

Old Friend and Khuya sneered at each other, then took Ursula back from me. Old Friend went first, embracing Ursula and regurgitating green slog into her mouth. As Old Friend did this, Khuya closed his eyes and the obsidian muscles covering his massive frame rippled as his four cocks swelled to engorged. One at a time he grasped each cock in his hand, working it until he spurted dark brown semen into Ursula's mouth. She gargled on both Old Friend's and Khuya's fluids until she sputtered awake and vomited the whole mess over the floor in a rank slurry.

"Uh, thanks," I said to Old Friend and Khuya.

Now wide awake but still pliant, Ursula allowed me to guide her out of her hospital room and back to the service elevator. We were able to waltz out of the busy hospital undetected. Most who saw us probably assumed I was taking Ursula outside for a cigarette. Some might have wondered if we were absconding. None cared.

As promised, Liza had the car outside the back door. Aamon was riding shotgun, which was good. No need for him to be in the backseat with his ailing mother, who looked like death barely warmed over and smelled like a mixture of vomit and semen.

I buckled Ursula in, and she promptly leaned her head against the cool glass of the window and fell asleep. I got in beside her and propped her head up with a spare blanket we had on the back seat. Liza handed me a plastic bag, should Ursula get sick on the ride.

"Is she gonna be okay?" Aamon asked as we pulled out of the parking lot.

"I don't know," I said.

His eyes grew wide and glossed over with the sheen of tears.

"Yes," Liza said, the word a blade. "She's going to be just fine, honey. People get sick, but the hospital gave her medicine to get better."

"She doesn't look better," Aamon said.

"She will," Liza assured him, emphasizing her lie by ruffling Aamon's hair.

Whether he believed it or not, he resigned himself to looking out the windshield and asking no more questions. I scolded myself for being so harsh with the boy. Perhaps he was just a child, and I needn't be so cold with him. Not everything and everyone was a demon, witch, or mixture like me.

Chapter Fourteen

Ursula vomited on the gravel as soon as I opened the car door. We'd pulled right up to her cabin again to save her from walking, which turned out to be a good thing. She was in no shape to do much but sleep.

"Right mess, she is," Marie said. "What did the docs have to say?"

"They said she should have stayed," Liza said as she shot me a burning side-eye.

"Her arm is stitched up," I said, "and she had IV antibiotics."

"Got more?" Marie asked.

I shook my head.

Marie sighed. "I got some back stock. What'd they give her?"

"Erythromycin," I said.

"Ugh," Marie said. "That'll give her tummy troubles, but I suppose that's the least of her worries."

Pretty sure the witch bile and demon seed were what

made her sick.

"Can you give her something for the nausea?" I asked. "The antibiotics are wreaking havoc, as are the withdrawals."

"Right MESS!" Marie emphasized. "I'll come up with a cocktail. Some Gravol, more antis, and Tylenol 3s for the pain. We'll get her through this but it's gonna be nasty."

"I need someone to supervise her, so she gets better and something like this," I said, motioning to her bandaged arm, "doesn't happen again."

"We can do shifts," Marie said. "Mojo and Merle can help."

"I will too," Liza said.

"You're good with kids," I said. "Could you mind Aamon?"

Liza shook her head. "I think maybe you and Aamon should spend some time together," she said. "Get to know one another."

Ah. Liza was a great many things, intelligent most of all. She wanted to get to the root of all of this, and Aamon might be the key. Ursula was certainly in no shape to shed light.

"Okay. So, I'll leave Ursula in your care, then," I said. "Aamon can come with me."

The boy appeared at my side.

"What are we gonna do?" he asked in a small voice.

He wasn't so cocksure after seeing Ursula in such a state. I offered him my hand and he took it, his grip tight.

Liza was grinning. I gave her a hard look, and she grinned even bigger. I wasn't good with kids, probably having never really been one myself. What I was good with was demons, witches, and all things other, and I strongly felt Aamon belonged in one of those categories.

Liza and Marie shuffled Ursula up the steps and into cabin four, and I led Aamon away toward the playground.

"Where are we going?" he asked.

"The playground," I said.

Aamon's face brightened.

"I can play?" he asked.

"Of course," I said.

It took us no time to get to the playground with Aamon having a new spring in his step. As soon as we were close, he wriggled out of my grasp and bounded off to play, choosing the teeter-totter to start with.

"Hey, kiddo," I called out. "You're gonna need two for …"

Oh.

He had another kid to balance out the teeter totter. Lavo was already perched on the opposing seat. When Aamon crawled into his seat, he lifted her in the air. He pushed off with all his might, and Lavo came bouncing down, all giggles and smiles. Then she pushed off and he came down, and up and down they went, their laughter a chorus with the ghosts of the kids of Eden that crawled over the jungle gym like ants.

I took a seat on the bench at the edge of the playground and watched them play. They bounced up and down as the ghost children played on the other equipment. I wondered if Aamon questioned why the swings were swinging and the merry-go-round was spinning. Or could he see the children? What did he think they were?

"C'mon!" Aamon called out. "Let's swing! Race ya!"

Aamon jumped off the teeter-totter and Lavo crashed to the ground. He already had a head start by the time she got to her feet, easily beating her to the swing set. He stood to the side and waited his turn.

He could see them.

Once the little ghost child jumped off, Aamon jumped on and started pumping his legs.

"Highest one is king of the playground!" he called.

Lavo crawled onto the swing beside him and pumped

her legs, leaning her whole body too and fro to gain momentum. As she leaned forward on her swing seat, I saw something sticking to her dress. Looked like gum, the way it stretched, but lots of it. And it was dark, almost black.

"Lavo," I said. "Your dress."

She and Aamon were too busy trying to win the crown to pay me any mind. I looked at the teeter-totter where Lavo had been seated. It was covered in the same dark substance. I walked closer and saw that it was all over the seat and the handles. I looked back to Lavo, at her blackened hands wrapped around the chains of the swing.

I touched the sticky substance on the seat of the teeter-totter. It was hot, and both slimy and tacky. It stuck to my palms and pulled away like thick, black spiderwebs. I tried to wipe my hands together, but it just spread the mess. I dropped to my knees and wiped my hands on the grass, and that's when I saw the footprints leading into the woods. No, not into the woods. *From* the woods, and the footprints were the same black sludge that now coated my hands, the seat of the teeter-totter, and the chains of the swing.

"You," I said.

I turned to look at Lavo on the swing, but she was standing overtop of me, her palms held open for me to see.

"It's rotten," she said. "It rots."

"What rots, Lavo?" I asked.

"Time," she said.

Her hands sizzled and the skin started melting away in gooey droplets of black pitch, leaving only boney digits like the ones I had beneath my gloves.

"And you," she said.

"Me?" I said.

"You're rotting," she said.

The next voice that came out of her throat was a cawing of crows and the braying of hounds.

"Half breed, tainted, rotten bitch!" the crows and

hounds said from deep within her belly.

"Lavo?"

Aamon was standing beside us, looking at Lavo with his brows scrunched. "Are we gonna keep playing?"

Her face relaxed and her lips curled into a little peach smile.

"Last one to the monkey bars is a rotten egg!" she taunted.

And off they ran, Lavo leaving footprints of rot on the grass.

Chapter Fifteen

The campers would be arriving soon. Four bookings this weekend. Two RVs and two tenters. The RVs had kids with them, and the tenters were couples, one with a child. With everything going on I wanted to cancel the bookings, but Marie convinced me that there was no reason to lose money.

"I honestly don't give a shit," I said. "I don't care if we ever have anyone here again."

Marie scrunched her face, her bushy grey brows unifying.

"Enough of you," she scolded. "Can't hide like a hermit."

"I'm not hiding like a hermit," I said. "I live here."

"Like a HERMIT," Marie said. "A goddamn shut in. You need people, Anna."

"People don't need me," I said. "I'm a blight."

Marie rolled her eyes and looked over at Liza.

"Has she been moping like this for long?" Marie asked.

Liza looked into her tea for an answer.

"You're moping too, I see," Marie said.

Marie had showed up at Eden's Edge with a U-Haul shortly after we took possession, with all her trinkets, elixirs, and books in tow. She was maternal, wise, and full of confident snark. She was exactly what I needed.

No, what I needed was my mom. But I was grateful to have Marie in my life.

We sat in Marie's cabin, covered from ceiling to floor in talismans, bones, flowers, and tomes on every wall, surface, and in every corner. It was unrestrained chaos but somehow felt cozy and safe. And Marie made the best tea, though I wondered if she was dosing it with something to take the edge off. Fuck knows Liza and I needed it.

"Listen here, you slits," Marie said. Lovingly, of course. "You've been through it, repeatedly. This is no different."

"What do you think is happening this time?" I asked.

"No fucking clue," Marie said.

The door opened and a breeze entered. The door remained open, and Marie crossed her arms.

"Come in or don't, ye ole hag," she said.

Miss Mojo entered, one fly at a time, until they were a swirling, buzzing horde that shaped themselves into a robust woman.

"Such a spectacle," Marie scolded.

"You's just jealous of what I can do," Miss Mojo said.

Now fully formed, skin and all, Miss Mojo took a seat in the lush rocker in the corner.

"That's my spot," Marie barked.

"You ain't in it," Miss Mojo said.

"I was gonna be," Marie said.

"*Gonna* and *is* are two different things," Miss Mojo said, crossing her arms across her massive breasts. "I *am* in it, and you're *gonna* be once I'm not."

I loved the way these two got on. Like the feisty aunts I

never had.

Or maybe I did have aunts. I never knew any family besides Mom and Dad, and I barely knew them at all.

"There she is," Marie said as she smiled my way. "I saw the twinkle of a smile before it soured into nostalgia there."

"We *are* your aunties," Miss Mojo said, knowing my mind. "And we love you. Both of you."

Liza smiled, but it was a Band-Aid over sadness. She was well and truly broken, and I had done that.

"No, you didn't," Miss Mojo said. "Life did that to her. To both of you."

Liza's brow furrowed in confusion as she looked between Mojo, Marie, and me.

"They're in my head," I said. "It's a witch thing."

"Ah," Liza said.

"Don't need to be in your head," Miss Mojo said. "Your sour is written all over your damn face."

"What else should I be?" I said. "Everything is going to shit again."

"Ah yes," Marie said. "The crux of the issue. Let's get to it, then."

"Tea?" Miss Mojo said.

Marie grimaced. "Like you like it?"

"Is that a problem?" Miss Mojo asked.

"It sure as hell is," Marie grumbled as she disappeared into the kitchen.

Miss Mojo was a bug witch. She commanded bugs, used bugs to manifest her spirit into living form, and liked all the things that bugs liked. Including decomp tea. Marie appeared moments later with a cup and saucer in one hand, pinching her nose with the other.

"It's not that bad," Miss Mojo said. "And I love you for indulging me."

Marie set the tea down and gave Miss Mojo a loving swat on the arm.

"Okay, Anna, catch me up," Miss Mojo said.

I told them everything, from my late-night grave naps, to the appearance of Old Friend, to the birth of an actual baby in my bathroom while Aamon watched on. I told them about Gus, about Lavo, and about the rot stemming from the lychgate. Rot that now blotched at least a dozen spots on my body.

"Let me see," Marie said.

I pulled up my pant leg, revealing the mass of black beneath.

"Looks to me like a clump of veins," Miss Mojo said. "Does it itch or feel hot?"

"No," I said. "I don't notice it unless it catches my eye."

"Hmmm," Marie said. "You said it started in only a few patches. Now it's spreading?"

"Not spreading, exactly," I said. "Appearing in more spots. They don't connect, though."

"Off with those clothes," Miss Mojo said, motioning her arms up into the air.

"Show you all of them?" I said.

"If you are comfortable with that," Marie said.

Everyone looked at Liza.

"I'm good with it," she said, but her voice was small. Wavering. Barely there.

Marie, Miss Mojo, and I had all sort of eyes and senses that Liza did not. We were less horrified by the truth of life and death. It gave me pause, but I knew this was for the best. I stripped down and stood in front of the three women, bare and exposed.

"Lift your breasts," Miss Mojo said.

I did. One at a time, slowly, turning to the side so they could see.

"Turn," Marie said.

I did, rotating slowly on the balls of my feet until my audience was back in front of me.

"Bend over," Miss Mojo said.

I did, and I spread my legs to give them a good look.

"Hmmmm," Marie said. "On your back?"

I laid on my back on the itchy rug. Marie knelt at my feet, and Miss Mojo heaved herself out of the chair to do the same. I tilted my head back just in time to see Liza leave the room.

"Let her go. It's a bit much for her," Marie said. "Now bring your knees to your chest and let them fall to the side."

I did as she asked.

"It's okay if we touch you?" Miss Mojo asked.

"Of course," I said.

"I'm going to spread your labia," Maria said. "Tell me of discomfort."

Their fingers went to work, examining my layers, scraping through hair, pressing around my rectum. It felt like thick spiders crawling over me, then inside me, their fingers examining and evaluating.

"You and Liza gettin' rough during sex?" Miss Mojo asked.

Liza coughed a wet sputter from the kitchen.

"No more than usual," I said. "Not all the time and not recently."

"In the past few weeks?" Miss Mojo asked.

I shook my head. "Few months back, maybe."

"There's trauma here," Miss Mojo said.

"All around," I murmured.

"I meant in your vagina," Miss Mojo snarked. "Marie, have a feel."

Marie's fingers were bonier than Miss Mojo's. Longer, too. They worked their way along my inner walls, kneading and prodding.

"Some tearing and bruising," Marie said. "Healing now, but still fairly fresh."

"Gus," I said. "And the … baby?"

"No birth," Marie said. "Not that much stretch and no evidence of tearing at the vaginal introitus. Perhaps a squirrel passed, but not the skull of a human babe."

"Gus came in parts," I said. "Mostly out of my guts and sinuses. Puke and snot, I believe. I assume his bones came out downstairs."

"There's no internal scraping like there was before," Marie said, recalling my sensory memories of Gus's first and subsequent births. "But there is something …"

Marie rooted deeper, her touch feeling like a cramp.

"Can you bear down?" Marie asked.

I did, and Miss Mojo massaged my abdomen and applied pressure.

"Sit up while I'm in you," Marie said.

I did, and when I was leaned onto the palm of her hand, I felt a gush between my legs.

"Got it," Marie said.

Miss Mojo released her pressure and Marie's hand evacuated my womb.

"I believe this is your territory," Marie said as she extended her hand to Miss Mojo. "Go freshen up, dear," she said to me. "Then we'll discuss."

I donned my clothes as the women chittered and chattered, examining their find. I cleaned myself up in the restroom, taking care to relieve myself after all that poking and prodding. After I was squared away, I went to the kitchen.

"Are they done with all that?" Liza asked.

She was standing over the sink, trying to drink her tea. Her hands were shaking so bad the liquid was sloshing out of the cup. I rested my hands on hers to steady both her and her tea, then helped bring the liquid to her lips.

"It doesn't bother me," I said of the examination.

"It bothers me," Liza said.

"I know," I said.

I released Liza's hand and let her drink the tea on her

own. Now was not the time to touch her. Seeing stuff like that reminded her of her childhood. Her violation.

She'd be better off dead.

I snarled. Liza turned and looked at me.

"My head voice," I said. "Speaking out of turn."

"Ladies?" Marie called.

"You stay," I said to Liza.

"I'd like to go home," she said.

"Of course," I said. "I'll be there in a bit."

Liza smiled. It was full of sorrow.

The back door clicked shut as I sat on the couch.

"Liza leave?" Marie asked.

My silence was answer enough.

"Dermestid beetles," Miss Mojo said.

She opened her hand, revealing the large flat insects within.

"Same as was in Lavo the first night I saw her in the woods," I said. "When I tore her in half."

"Yeah. Same as in your buried jar. I looked for 'em after you tol' me where to dig. Seems these little critters have a particular fondness for dried animal matter," Miss Mojo said. "Quite often museums, universities, and taxidermists use these to clean specimens without causing any damage. They focus on the meat and tissue without cracking, warping, or discolouring bone."

"Are they dangerous?" I asked. "Were they eating me from the inside? Are they causing the rot?"

Miss Mojo shook her head. "They don't like it moist. People that use these little guys to clean carcasses dry their specimens first. Meat that's too wet can lead to mold and decay, which is lethal to these buggers."

"Then what does this mean?" I asked.

"They can be everywhere," Miss Mojo said. "Wherever there's a carcass, and fuck knows we got plenty of that round these woods. Moose, birds, rodents. These guys are nature's great cleansing crew."

"But why is this inside me?" I asked. "And why in Lavo? She was practically made of these things."

"Cleansing her?" Marie offered.

"From what?" Miss Mojo said.

I thought of the decay. "And it seems that Eden's Edge, and me, are rotting, not getting cleaner."

"Ah ah," Marie said, waggling a finger at me. "Rot is not bad. Rot is cleansing, too, in its way."

"It kills living tissue," I argued. "Spreads like a virus."

"Making way for new life," Marie said.

"At the expense of the old," I said.

The discussion continued, but Marie's and Miss Mojo's voices became a soft hum beneath the loud thoughts within my head. I zoned out, hearing my mom's voice, my dad's growl, the flap of Erinyes's wings, the skitter of Gus's claws, the thump of Old Man Merle's single yellow boot. Did all of that need to be cleansed in order to save Eden?

A song interrupted my thoughts.

Anna Anna quite contrary …

The window was open. Marie's beaded curtains danced in the night breeze.

How does your garden grow?

I stood, and Marie and Miss Mojo stopped speaking.

"Go," Miss Mojo said to me. "Whatever you're hearing, follow."

My lip quivered and the inside of my throat thickened.

"I'm scared," I said.

The women both stood. Each took one of my hands.

"Yes," they said in unison. No, not in unison, in a *trio*, my mom's voice joining theirs. "You are smart, and you are strong."

I followed the nursery rhyme into the black of night.

Chapter Sixteen

Lavo walked the path in front of me, her steps light, airy, innocent. I knew she was not any of those things, though. There was a heaviness to her, a darkness. Witch? Demon? Neither. She wasn't real. She lived somewhere beyond, somewhere I had yet to tread.

After exiting Marie's house, Lavo's song had reduced to a hum in her throat, two voices braided into one, an alto and a soprano. It was equal parts enchanting and wretched. I found myself humming along though I did not know the tune, and yet I hit every note in the correct place, every pitch, every wax and wane.

We approached my house and Lavo stopped. I stopped, too, watching her closely as she did a pirouette on the balls of her feet, stopping on the fourth rotation to face me. Her smile was tight and fluid, like something in her lips was finagling them into shape.

"What hell do you bring me?" I asked her.

"What hell have you brought?" she replied, her voices

two at once.

I was in no mood for riddles.

"I don't know what you are," I said, "but I know I don't want you here."

Lavo responded with a giggle, and her eyes glowed, one blue, one black. Fire crackled within the black eyes, embers resting on her lashes and crackling on her pallid cheek. She lowered herself to the ground and tucked her legs beneath herself. The gravel on the road pierced the skin on her knees and black pitch oozed out. She held eye contact with me as she lifted her hand to her lips and kissed it, licked it, then bit into the flesh. Blood trickled out of the corners of her mouth as she chewed, swallowed, then tore off another bite.

"Hungry?" I asked.

"Grmphh," she said through a mouthful of meat.

Laughter like birdsong trilled from behind my house. Giggles I didn't recognize. Female, wheezing, broken.

Lavo had wrapped her ankle behind her head, hiked up her skirt, and was now dining on the inside of her thigh. Good, juicy meat, that. I left her in a pile of blood and shredded flesh as I crept along my garden to my backyard.

Erinyes and Gus were perched high in a tree, Gus chittering to her as he watched the scene below. I wondered if he was describing to her what was transpiring, and wished he could tell me, too. I had no desire to look. I knew whatever it was was going to be unpleasant.

"Liza?" I said, knowing full-well it wasn't her. Liza would not be out here in the middle of the night. Liza would not be laughing. I had heard her laugh so little in life, and certainly not in the past week.

My greeting was answered with another giggle, and a huff of air that sounded like attempted speech. I had already announced my presence, so I strode around the house like I belonged. Mary was there on the corner of the deck, head bobbing and shoulders heaving.

"Mary!" I said. "Who brought you out here?"

It was late, and the mosquitos were thick, as were the wolves and mountain cats just outside the yard. She should not be out here on her own. Why would Liza have …

But Mary was not alone. As I got closer, walking a wide berth into the yard so I could see her from the front, I spotted a hand in hers. The hand was long and grey, nails rotted and black. Though the fingers were stretched to an unnatural length, the knuckles were young and soft. Another step, and I could see a stretched-taffy arm leading to a thin, ropey body and a mess of dark hair.

"Laz," I gasped.

He wasn't screaming, as had been his way since his death. His mouth was open, but the corners were curled up in a kind of sloppy smile. Mary held his hand and they chatted, language made of chirps, gargles, and wheezes. They giggled in dissonant unison, then Laz embraced her, his stretched arms reaching around her whole body and hand rested on his own back. When he pulled away, I could see the sheen of their tears glistening in the moonlight.

This was the first I'd seen Laz move from where he hung out. This was the first I'd heard his screams silenced, replaced by something sounding like joy. My throat clenched with a sob and I pressed my hand over my hearts as I watched them catching up on all those years lost. My tears of joy turned to confusion as Laz took Mary by the hands and guided her out of her wheelchair.

Mary walked like she'd never been chair bound in the first place. Her hair thickened into heavy curls that cascaded down her back like a waterfall. Her clothes sloughed off as she and Laz walked arm and arm into the yard. But she wasn't naked, and neither was he. She was wearing a sheer, beaded wedding dress, and him, a pale silver suit. They danced under a canopy that was laced with ivy and fairy lights. The yard, my yard, was abuzz with the glow of a wedding reception, the romantic tunes of a string quartet, the chiming of people's laughter, and the clinking of champagne glasses.

"What …"

The sound of my voice caused everything to dissolve. Mary crumpled to the ground, her wedding dress replaced by the flannel nightgown that Liza and I had bought her. Laz was there, but he was hanging mid air again, his arms extended in invisible crucifixion.

"Why?" Mary mewled. "Why!"

I was pleased to hear her voice again, but not so happy to hear her pain.

"Why what?" I stammered as I walked toward her.

"Why save me?" she screamed, saliva flying from her mouth as she spat the words at me. "You should have let me die!"

"I couldn't kill you," I said, breathless, crying.

Mary's sobs ceased and her face cleared of all emotion. She spoke, and her voice was that of a child again.

"You watched him take me," she said, speaking of Bobby. "Do you know the things he did to me?"

I could imagine. I'd seen Liza chained up in that basement, and the damage inflicted, the blood on the floor … I still saw the scars today, both physical and emotional.

"You could have stopped him," she said.

"I didn't know," I said. "I didn't know what I was, what I could do."

Mary smiled. It was the most unnerving expression I'd seen on someone's face. Beside her, Laz smiled too, a black hollow shape framed with lips like bloated blue worms.

"You know *now*," they said in unison. "Save us, Anna. Save us!"

They continued chanting, and other voices joined in, chanting from all around. Familiar voices from years past.

Miss Mojo. Old Man Merle. Mom.

The dead people in Vancouver, the ones the cops

thought I killed.

The children of Eden's Edge who perished at Allison's hand.

Mr. Charles, the other residents, Robbie Cum Crocs, Kaz.

Everyone who I'd ever been in contact with was now chanting at me, their voices gnarled and sour.

Save us

Save us

Save us

"I can't," I said. "I can't take it back, any of it."

The chanting continued, peppered with staccato giggles and screeches that hurt my head. I dropped to my knees and covered my ears, and in my head, I heard the chitter of Gus and the chirp of Erinyes.

Save us, they seemed to say.

"Fuck off!" I screamed.

And they did. Everything went silent, even the squirrel and bird. I opened my eyes and looked at Mary. She was facedown in the grass in front of her wheelchair like someone had tipped her forward. She turned her head to face me.

"You're right," she said, her voice a strangled rasp. "You aren't strong enough. You are only two halves, not worth shit."

Mary laughed and black blood poured from her nose and mouth.

"Fog and steam,

Gossamer and Pitch

Halfbreed Tainted rotten bit—"

Her last word was cut off by the rattle of death, her pupils shrinking to pin pricks, leaving her eyes as pale as Laz's ghost.

"No, no, NO!" I screamed.

I scrambled over to Mary and turned her on her side. I felt her neck for a pulse, checked her mouth for breathing, but there was nothing.

I started CPR. The black sludge coating her mouth tasted like soot and curdled milk, but I pushed on. I had to save her this time. I could save her. I was smart, and I was strong, and …

"Anna, what the fuck?"

Liza came barreling out the door, phone in hand.

"9-1-1," I said between rescue breaths.

I kept going while Liza frantically explained to the person on the other end what was going on. I was still breathing, pumping, breathing when the trees lit up with flashing red, and the sound of the sirens wailed like banshees in the night, heralding Mary's death.

Chapter Seventeen

I couldn't save her. Not when she was a child being brutalized and stolen from Eden's Edge, not as an adult in my care. The ambulance had come with a vengeance and left with little fanfare. Mary's death was pronounced on the scene. There was nothing they could do for her.

Nothing *I* could do for her.

Mary was in my care, so I approved an autopsy. I wanted to know what finally caused her body to give out. The black blood I saw was not an illusion. The paramedics asked about it, as did Liza. I'd ingested mouthfuls of it from giving her CPR. Upon close inspection by the medics, neither Mary nor I were bleeding from anywhere they could see. The police came alongside the paramedics, of course, and scoured the scene. Nothing looked untoward, so they, too, awaited the results of the autopsy. Though no one looked concerned. Mary had suffered many health issues for many years, and they figured her death was related to one of those.

I wasn't convinced.

"What do you mean she walked into the yard?" Liza asked as she placed a cup of coffee in my hand.

I was grateful for the coffee. After everyone had left, I showered away the blood of Mary and three layers of my skin before coming out to sit on the patio. My hair was wet and I was cold. I grasped the coffee, trying to press as much of my flesh against the mug as I could.

"She seemed to be talking to …"

I couldn't tell Liza. Couldn't tell her that her friend that had been tortured and murdered in front of her as a child was still residing here in Eden's Edge.

"… someone," I lied. "And then she just got out of her chair and walked into the yard."

"How?" Liza asked.

"I don't know," I said. "But … I saw other things, too."

Liza was going to ask a question, but she stayed quiet, her eyes fixed on me.

"She was in a wedding dress," I said. "And she danced, and she spoke, and she was so, so happy. Then it all changed."

"Her wheelchair was in the yard," Liza said.

It was. Now it was back on the porch, parked where Mary used to sit every morning when the sun rose and the birds began their daily song.

"I don't know how it got there," I said.

"It didn't move itself," Liza said.

I gritted my teeth. "Are you suggesting I moved it?'

"Maybe you don't remember," Liza said. "You've been out of sorts lately."

"I have?" I said, my voice an octave higher than I intended. "Things have got to shit again, and you know, *we* know, the worst is coming. I'm not out of sorts, Liza. The world fucking is."

"Your world," she said under her breath.

Her words were a slap. I was different; I knew that. But

I never considered that everything happening was only happening to me. I was the only one who could see it, hear it, feel it. Until innocent people got killed.

"I'm sorry," she said. "I didn't mean it so rough. I believe you see what you see, and that the things you tell me are happening are real. But all I really experience is your strain, your pain. And then the deaths …"

Liza hesitated and placed her hand on her stomach.

"I'm sorry," I said.

I put my coffee on the little table beside the porch swing and tried to take Liza's hands, but she pushed me away.

"Liza, c'mon, I—"

But she wasn't angry. She was sick. She leapt off the porch swing, fell to her knees at the edge of the patio, and vomited in a violent stream over the yard. She vomited a second time before I could even reach her.

"It's okay," I said as I held her black hair out of her face and rubbed her back. "I've got you."

She vomited once more before wiping her mouth with the back of her hand and curling up on her side.

"Let's get you inside," I said.

"I still feel sick," she said, punctuating that with a belch.

"I'll get you a bowl."

I helped Liza inside and into the bed. Her whole body was cold but slick with sweat, and her hair was stuck to her face in stringy black webs. All I could think about was the black blood on Mary lips and tried to remember if any had gotten on Liza.

"Just something I ate," she murmured as she pulled the blanket up to her chin. "Or stress."

"Stress," I said, nodding.

I sat beside Liza and stroked her hair.

"Beautiful," Lavo said from the ensuite. "It has begun."

My head snapped in her direction.

"Fuck off," I said.

"What?" Liza mumbled, but her eyes were fluttering.

"A second chance," Lavo said. "To save them."

I didn't respond, mostly because I didn't want to disturb Liza.

"Save everyone," Lavo repeated. "Save yourself."

"I don't know how," I whispered.

"Because you are not whole," she said.

"I am who I am," I said.

Halfbreed tainted rotten bitch.

"You ruined it," Lavo said.

"Ruined what?" I asked.

Tears were rolling down my face. I knew what I had ruined. I ruined everything with my inaction. Mary, Laz, Liza. Mom.

"*You're* ruined," Lavo said, her voice sing song. "Spoiled meeeeeaaaatttt."

Dermisted beetles poured from Lavo's mouth, riding on her vowels. She belched, but no air passed. Only clumps and blobs of beetles that poured to the floor in great waves. She strained and farted, and beetles poured from the bottom of her dress. So many beetles, a brown blight, and they spread across the floor like a slick of old blood. I lifted my feet onto the bed, but they crawled up the footboard by the hundreds until the duvet was a blanket of shimmering carapaces. The more I brushed them off or kicked them away, the more crawled up from the carpet.

Lavo gasped a breath when there was a reprieve in the flow of beetles from her mouth.

"Let them cleanse," she said.

The beetles were all over Liza, all over me. They crawled into her mouth and ears, into all my holes. Their feet tickling and mouths pinching.

"Let them," Lavo said.

I had no choice but to let them. I was pinned in place by the sheer weight of the beetles. My head was turned to the side, so I had a full view of every nip of meat they chewed off Liza. She was blissfully unaware, her eyes still beneath her lids, her lips pursed and blowing tiny snores around the penetrating beetles.

No.

"No!" I screamed, sending a projectile clump of beetles out of my mouth to strike Lavo in the face. I wiped, swiped, stood, and jumped up and down to rid myself of the coating of bugs. Once I could move freely, I ripped the duvet off the bed and fanned Liza with it. The beetles blew away or scattered, leaving only the ones inside her. I scooped them from her mouth, plucked them from her ears, and rolled her on her back so I could extract them from her vagina. But when I lowered her panties, I found no beetles.

"No death to cleanse," Lavo said.

Not a single beetle. Not inside of her, that I could tell, and not in the slit of her ass or the crease of her groin. But her belly was distended and misshapen. I pressed it and it shifted.

"They're inside of her," I said, panic taking hold. "Get them out!"

Lavo giggled and hiccuped, and a single dermisted beetle launched out of her nose.

I didn't know what to do. I couldn't dig into Liza to clean the beetles out without hurting her, and I didn't even think it was possible to get them, deep as they were.

"Erinyes!" I yelled at the window, which was slightly ajar.

After a few moments she arrived, first striking the window a few times before landing on the sill.

"Get Mojo," I said. "Or Marie. Or both!"

Without hesitation, Erinyes took wing, leaving in a streak of red across the sky. I massaged Liza's stomach, and she groaned in response.

"I'm sorry," I said.

"About everything," Lavo said in my voice. Then, in a

different voice. My mom's voice. "Save them. Save yourself."

"Fuck you!" I bellowed, and Liza cried out.

Lavo was gone, and Liza was sitting up on the bed, fighting against the pressure of my hands, which judging by the red marks on her abdomen was way too hard.

"I'm sorry," I said as I gently placed my hands atop hers, which were rested on her belly. "Did I hurt you?"

"No," she said, breathless, "I don't think—"

She vomited over herself, me, and the blanket. It was black as pitch and swirling like oil.

"Mojo is coming," I said, to both myself and her. "Marie."

As if summoned by the devil, the two of them burst into the bedroom, Marie through the door and Miss Mojo in a swarm through the crack in the window.

"Out," Marie commanded.

"No, I want to sta—"

"Out!" Marie repeated.

Miss Mojo constituted into her human self and the ladies got to work on Liza, poking, prodding, examining. I took my leave, giving Liza the same privacy she'd offered me when the ladies did my own examination out in the living room. When I reached the kitchen, Liza cried out, and I heard the squelch of vomit purge from her body once again. My talons cut through my knuckles. What was I going to do? Run in there slashing and hacking?

I ran outside, into the yard, back into the woods and collapsed on the loam. I cried, my body wracking with sobs and the ground soaking in my tears. I ripped away my clothing and lay prone in the dirt, pressing the cool forest floor into my flesh. I lay there, panting, trying to home in on the sounds of the forest when something tickled my side.

"Gus," I said.

I missed Gus's tail. It was fluffy and soft against my

skin. Now I had the smoothness of the fur on his face, but the tough bones of his spine scraped me as he circled four times and lay down on the small of my back. Erinyes was next, nestling into the tangle of my hair, fluffing it into a nest with her feet before settling in.

Old Man Merle came last, sitting on a nearby log with a pair of spoons.

"Play for me," I said to Merle.

And he did. He launched into jigs and reels that danced off those spoons, echoing off the trees, as I tried to push thoughts of Liza from my mind.

Chapter Eighteen

I was asleep with my face pressed into a patch of bramble when Miss Mojo buzzed out to retrieve me.

"Come on, girlie," she said as she slid her hands into my armpits and hoisted me to my feet.

I leaned on her; my face squished into the side of her breast as she led me to the house. Once inside, I veered toward the hallway, but she steered me toward the living room and the couch.

"I want to see Liza," I said.

"I know," she said. "But we need to talk."

It was serious. I knew, because Marie was already on the couch, hands folded in her lap.

"What's wrong?" I asked.

"Sit," Marie said. She patted the couch beside her.

"Is Liza okay?" I asked.

"Yes," Miss Mojo said. She wasn't as gentle as Marie. She plunked me down on the center cushion beside Marie and sat down on the other cushion beside me. Since I was still naked, they wrapped me in my crocheted blanket. Not that I felt shame.

"Now listen," Marie said as she took one hand. Miss Mojo already had a firm grip on the other. "Liza is fine. She's alive, and she's calm. In fact, she's sleeping."

"Did you give her something to knock her out?" I asked.

"Of course I did," Marie said. "I gave her a cocktail of Lion's Mane mushroom and hops. I would have used fly agaric, but there's too big a risk with a smattering of toxins."

"You used that on me, when we first met," I said.

Marie nodded. "I did. But you weren't …"

Marie and Miss Mojo exchanged a look I didn't quite care for.

"I wasn't what?" I asked. "What's going on?"

Miss Mojo squeezed my hand. Marie sighed.

"Liza's pregnant."

My stomach braided itself into knots.

"No,'" I said.

"Yes," Marie said.

Erinyes came to the window, her wings beating the glass. Everywhere her feathers struck she left a black smudge. Her feathers were gummy with rot.

"Who'd she fuck?" I asked, knowing full well she didn't fuck anyone.

Anyone but me.

"No one," Miss Mojo said. "No one *else*. I don't know how, I don't know why, but …"

Gus joined Erinyes at the window. His fur and bones were clean—no black pitch—but his eyes were oozing the stuff in fat drops that plopped onto the windowsill. Gus reached up for Erinyes with his paws, drawing her in and hugging her so she'd stop smashing against the window.

They'd been together for oh so long. A lifetime to them, and beyond.

"It's mine," I said. "The baby."

Miss Mojo and Marie stared at each other for a beat before turning their attention back to me.

"Feels that way," Marie confirmed. "Though there's no way to know for sure."

I had no penis, no testicles, no sperm. But the last time Liza and I fucked, I released into her. I felt it, and so did she. She filled me and I filled her in return. It made no sense, and yet it was.

I didn't know what else to say. Neither did they. We sat on the couch in silence. Miss Mojo released my hand so she could rub my back, and I rested my head against Marie's shoulder.

"What do we do now?" I asked.

"We wait," Marie said. "She is progressing quickly. More than a … normal pregnancy should."

Liza's belly was so distended, so suddenly.

"It's like an alien," I said.

"Or a demon," Miss Mojo offered.

"Or witch," Marie countered.

Halfbreed, tainted, rotten bitch.

"I don't want that," I said. "I wish I could take the best parts of me and give only those to Liza. Leave out Khuya, my father, completely."

"Difficult to say which traits a babe will inherit," Miss Mojo said. "Bit of each, usually."

Lavo's words were an ear worm that chattered in my brain, over and over and over.

You are not whole.

Save them

Save them

saVe tHEm …

I shook my head to rid myself of the noise. It almost worked, but Lavo's voice remained, a grey hum in the back of my mind.

"Prenatal care?" I asked.

"I can provide what she needs," Marie said. "Doctors wouldn't understand. And they might not be able to help, once the time comes."

Birth. What would it be? Witch? Demon?

Halfbreed—

"Shhhhhh," I told myself. "All I want is Liza to be safe."

Safe wasn't enough. I wanted her happy. Content, at the least.

"I'll make sure she's comfortable," Marie said.

That wasn't much of a promise. Comfortable is what you offered people in palliative care.

"I would like to see her," I said.

They didn't argue, though the expression on their faces said they wanted me to do anything but. I had to see her, though. I did this to her. All of it.

I was a ghost floating down the hall, reaching the bedroom door before I realized my feet were even on the floor. Liza was on her back on the bed staring out the window, a thin satin sheet laid delicately over her body. She was naked. I could see every bump and curve, including the dimples of her nipples and the roundness of her breasts. And the enormous mound where her flat belly had once been.

"Anna."

While I'd been staring at her belly, Liza had turned her head from the window. She was staring into me with those wide, black eyes.

"I felt it, you know," she said. "I didn't know what it was, but you came in me. I could feel every milliliter. I didn't know what it was, but you filled me, and it was so warm and good. And then I came, and it drew further up inside me, and that's where it stayed. The feeling never went away."

I sat on the bed beside her, and she took my hand and placed in on her belly.

"This is so fucking weird," I said.

She laughed. The sound was music.

"I didn't realize you were so much of a dick that you could become one," she said.

I laughed, and then we were crying. I laid down beside her and draped my leg over hers while embracing her belly.

"Why are you naked?" she asked.

"I ripped off all my clothes in the woods and laid down in the dirt," I said. "Took a little nap."

I circled her erect nipple with my finger. "Why are you naked?" I asked.

"So your witchy duo could finger me," she said. "Or rather, fist me. At least that's what it felt like."

"Yeah," I said. "They'll do that."

We laughed again and pulled each other close.

There was no way of knowing how any of this would end. I wanted to believe it would end well, and that we would emerge from this madness with a baby in our arms and in our home, and we would grow old and watch her graduate, marry, have babies of her own. I wanted so badly to believe.

"We'll get through this," Liza said. She couldn't read my mind, but she could feel my tension. She always could.

"I love you," I said.

"I love you," she replied.

We kissed. It was wet, warm velvet. She ran her hand down my arms, stroking me with her fingertips, but abruptly stopped when she reached my elbow.

"What happened?" she asked.

I contorted my arm to get a look. Could have been dirt, those black lines like thick veins creeping up the back of my arm. I might have convinced her of that—I'd slept on the forest floor, after all. But honesty was important. She and I both needed that.

"Rot," I said. "It's spreading."

Her expression was blank. I pulled away from her and stood in front of the window, on display.

Liza scrutinized every centimeter of me. Got to her

knees on the bed, her fingertips exploring my skin. The black pitch has spread in tendrils from my thighs to my hips, across my left breast and into my armpit, on the backside of each arm. And one of my feet was entirely black with the thickness of the veiny webbing.

"You're sick," she said. Breathless.

"No," I said. "I'm rotting."

"That's illness," she argued.

"It's decay," I said. "And Eden's Edge decays with me."

She sat back, her eyes finally meeting mine. "The lychgate."

"Yes," I said. "I'll figure it out. Start there. I … all those nights I wandered there, eating dirt. I picked up whatever taints the soil."

"A doctor …" she said but trailed off. She knew no doctor could help me or stop this. Doctors would lead to involuntary treatment orders, institutionalization. Ignorance was fear.

I placed my hand on Liza's stomach. It rippled under my touch.

"Fucking bizarre," she said.

The sheen of tears on her eyes … I wished it were happiness, and though there may have been some of that there, it was also fear, despair, panic, madness. I kissed her eyes, hoping to take the tears and absorb them into myself, but the moisture remained.

"We'll be okay," I lied.

Liza returned the lie with a kiss. "I know."

We were quiet for a spell, me sitting beside Liza, our hands entwined on her belly.

"Will we have a funeral?" Liza asked. "For Mary?"

I hadn't thought of that.

"Of course we will," I said. "Tonight. I'll have Merle start moving logs, get Marie to have some candles and flowers."

Liza nodded. There was suspicion in her eyes. I'd be suspicious of me, too. But I didn't kill Mary…

Didn't I?

"No, I didn't," I said.

Liza pulled away.

I wasn't so sure I hadn't killed Mary. Wheeled her out onto that lawn and suffocated her. And neither was Liza. Mary's corpse was wedged between us, joining all the other events as of late. I hoped we could grow past this and survive whatever plagued Eden's Edge. And me.

Chapter Nineteen

It was a lovely gathering. Eden's Edge would have been a splendid place for a wedding, were it not for the thick sense of dread that hung from the trees like gossamer, thick in the air like southern humidity. Even though it was night, even though most insects, birds, and animals would typically be asleep, they were all there as witness. Their eyes glowed shades of green and gold in the trees, the quiet rustling accompanying Merle's fiddle as he played a somber ballad.

Liza had cut all the blooms from my mom's rose bushes and spread them around the pyre Merle'd built earlier in the day. The white petals glowed like stars on the black ground, and the red ones matched Erinyes's feathers. Mary was dressed in yellow lace with matching high heels on her slender feet. She would have loved that. She'd always fancied being a princess, or at least an adult woman. She was laid out on the pyre, loonies on her eyes, her bloodstone clasped in her bound-together hands.

Gus was perched on my shoulder, Erinyes on the other, as the ghosts of Eden gathered around the pyre. The children flickered, grey and smooth, and the adults were barely-there specters like greasy spots in the air. Miss Mojo joined us as a flight of moths that hovered over Mary, ruffling her hair with the breeze off their wings. Marie stood nearby, a moss-green candle in her hand, its flame flickering in her eyes.

I didn't know what to say. There were so many words, but none seemed quite right. I had known Mary so briefly. And the Mary that had died on the lawn of Eden had truly died many years before at the hands of Bobby Pickton, but her body remained. I had hoped to save some part of Mary, to give her a taste of the life that had been stolen from her, but all I ended up doing was prolonging her death.

So no, I could not find words to say in memoriam as everyone was gathered around, their eyes on Mary's now peaceful body laid out beneath the stars.

Merle's ballad turned into a mournful requiem as Marie used her candle to light the dry brush stuffed between the logs of the pyre. The wood lit, and so did Mary, her hair coiling to her scalp as it burned away. Her flesh started to sizzle, and I couldn't help but think of those pigs on that farm all those years ago. I could still hear them oinking, snuffling through the dirt for food and bones …

The crowd had become larger. Much larger than it should have been. Before, there were the ghosts of Eden that had remained after Allison had murdered them. There were my magical familiars, my impossible friends, Marie, Kaz. There was also Aamon and Ursula, sitting side by side on the ground, looking rather bored with everything. But now there was a crowd that expanded out in rows to the edge of the tree line. Police officers I'd met from the city, patrons from the Crown and Anchor, Robbie Cum Crocs and the clerk from the mall. There was the waitress from Goats on the Roof, the ferry captain, the gas station attendant. The original waitress from the cafe where Mom and I had first met Allison, that night when we'd run away so long ago.

Everyone was there. Everyone that I'd met after I'd killed my dad. But they were off. Tainted. Rot grew on them like it grew on me, but theirs was actively chewing away flesh—ripping, tearing, and peeling until they were masses of exposed muscle, blood, and tissue. They swayed, singing along in a haunting choral melody to Merle's requiem as the ground shifted and a plague of dermisted beetles rose from the dirt. The beetles coated all the meat and fluids, devouring everything until new people emerged beneath. People that were smiling, laughing, wearing different clothes and less blood. Cops became nurses, waitresses became day traders and housewives. Extra laugh lines, longer hair, scars like roadmaps of adventures. New lives, fresh and clean.

A single voice wailed about the rest, a soprano howl that kept time with Merle's music. The crowd of new people parted and Laz walked forward, his mourning melody wailing from his throat. I backed away as his stretched body swayed like taffy with every step until he reached the pyre. He crawled on top of Mary, covering her, penetrating her and moving his hips until she gasped a breath. In that fire, he spurted inside her and her belly grew, round and slick, until their babe squelched out into the flame and ash. Once Mary's child was at her breast, Laz helped her off the logs and out onto the grass.

Not real, I told myself.

But it was lovely, nonetheless. All the newly exposed people were dancing, clinking drinks, toasting the happy couple. But it wasn't Mary and Laz's wedding, though they were dressed to the nines. Mary had a toddler on her hip and an older child by her side, and Laz and she both wore bands on their ring fingers. Already married.

Everyone tapped their glasses with forks coated in wedding cake.

"Speech!" they cried, laughing and clapping.

Who is making a speech? Whose wedding?

I spun to look at the pyre. It was now a stage of white roses contained within nets of fairy lights. Liza stood atop a stump, dressed in an all-lace gown, her hair cascading down her body in blue-black waves.

"Liza," I said, and she reached for me.

I tried to move, to walk to her, but my bare feet stuck to the ground. The rot had consumed my lower half, sealing me to the ground like tree sap. The more I struggled, the more the sap trailed in capillaries up my body until I couldn't move my arms, my neck, my head.

Liza was screaming. The front of her ivory dress had a red stain blooming below the pudge of her belly. She released an astounding wail, and blood gushed from her, staining the entire lower half of her dress and accumulating in a pond at her feet. The waterfall of blood became thick with globs of meat and chips of bone, and some fully formed organs—eyes, hearts, livers, ears. The eyes bounced and rolled, all of them watching me, all familiar eyes. I wanted to keep watching, horrid as it was, but my own rot crept over my eyes and formed a tacky shell over my corneas and beneath my lids. I wanted to claw at my face, to scream, but I was covered entirely in rot, even my tongue and the inside of my throat. Everything was dark and silent.

Until …

Tiny feet crawled across my face. My torso. Between my toes and on the back of my thighs.

The dermisted beetles worked away, gnawing in tiny chomps, ripping and stripping. Once my hands were free, I helped them by scratching and tearing away flaps of flesh until I was clean and new. My body was my own, only better, with unmarred skin, toned muscle, and a touch of extra height.

Liza was no longer on the pyre. The pyre was no longer

there. In its place stood Lavo and Aamon, hand in hand, smiling.

"What are you?" I asked, my volume crescendoing to a scream. "Why are you here?!"

The crowd had left. It was only Lavo, Aamon, and I in Eden's edge. There were no campers, no tents, not even the cabins. Not even my own home. But Old Friend's house still stood, though it was nothing but bones. A foundation and a mess of boards. The skeleton of a house half-erected.

Lavo and Aamon simultaneously opened their mouths, and a soulful vibrato rang through the trees. A harmonic chord that signaled the end of the requiem.

It wasn't them. It was Merle's strings.

You're losing it, Anna.

You are lost.

"Beautiful," Miss Mojo said of Merle's final note. Being dead herself, she could hear Old Man Merle's violin singing Mary's funeral songs. Only the dead and I could hear all the goings on at Eden's Edge.

Miss Mojo stood to my right with Marie, and Liza was on my left, arm linked in mine, hand on her belly. Her face glistened with tears.

Mary was burning. It was an open-air pyre, so she'd likely take about four hours or so to burn. But she was unrecognizable now. Each ghost and person in turn said their goodbyes, until Liza and I were the only ones left.

"I wish I remembered her only as a child," Liza said. "Playful, hopeful, pure joy."

"Yeah," I said.

I had nothing more to say. I'd apologize, but Liza had heard that. I wished I'd made different choices, but Liza had heard that, too.

"I wish we'd let her die," Liza said. "She could have been at peace long ago."

I agreed, but I didn't say so.

Liza tugged my arm and guided me back toward the house. Erinyes and Gus clung to my sweater, determined to accompany us the entire way.

Chapter Twenty

Liza and I slept in the next morning. I'd wanted to go for a walk after we got home, but she insisted I come to bed. There was enough tension between us, so I didn't push the matter. I'd never imagined I could fall asleep, with both my mind and body racing, but the night had been a blackout, dark and silent. Not even my dreams spoke to each other.

As we drifted into consciousness, we embraced.

I sat up.

"You're huge," I said.

Liza held her belly.

"Bigger," she said, "but not huge."

She was huge. Her belly had doubled in size overnight. I ran my finger along her linea nigra, and something beneath her flesh pressed back, pressing into the pad of my finger as I traced the line up and down.

Outside, gravel crunched beneath the weight of tires.

"Fuck," I said.

"Campers," she said out the window. "I forgot."

"Me too," I said.

"This isn't the best time," I grumbled. "But Marie wouldn't be convinced otherwise."

"I know," she said. "Business as usual."

I leaned in and kissed Liza again, then another time on her forehead.

"It's only a few days," I said. "It'll be low-key and quiet. The rot is thus far only at the cemetery—"

"And on you," Liza said, brushing her fingers over my abdomen.

"Yes, well, I will keep my distance from people, but also watch over the cemetery," I said. "But I won't be far. I'll be here in case anything happens."

I placed my hand on Liza's stomach. It rippled under my touch.

"I'm fine," she said.

But she was anything but. Her eyes were panicked, like prey at the teeth of a predator. Madness lingered there, threatening to push her over the edge. The sheen of tears on her eyes … I wish it were happiness, and though there may have been some of that there, it was also fear, despair, panic.

"Sleep," I said, and I covered her up.

I left the room, giving a quick nod to Kaz who stood sentry in the corner, Erinyes on his shoulder. He would send her for me if Liza needed anything.

Eden's Edge was bustling with activity.

"Gahhhh."

Old Man Merle stood at the edge of the forest, watching over the new people. The campers had arrived throughout the morning and were pert near set up. One RV showed up, hauling a family of four complete with a dog, bikes, and all sorts of infant gear. The other three groups were tenters—a solo female, two dudes, and a group of three teens. It was a lot of people to keep track of, but we kept the RV close to the tenting stage, so no one was off on their own. I couldn't control where they wandered, but at night people tended to stay close to light and other heartbeats.

"It'll be okay, Merle," I said.

His face suggested he believed otherwise. He was sullen and twitchy, jumping at every noise and movement. I put my hand on his and gave him a squeeze.

"If you feel comfortable, can you hang out here?" I asked. "Keep an eye on the woods between Eden and the cemetery? I don't think the rot is spreading that fast, and I'm pretty sure those creatures were barred in when I tipped the lychgate, but I'd like to be sure. Holler if anything looks sideways over here."

"Gahhhh," Merle said as he pointed a broken, skeletal finger at the visiting campers.

"I'll watch them," I said. "As will Kendra, Miss Mojo, and Marie."

Merle's upper lip curled into a smile, but his eye sockets drooped with sadness. He touched my belly then pointed toward my house.

"Oh yes," I said. "I'll be keeping the closest eye on her."

Merle seemed satisfied with that and disappeared into the woods. I was confident that he would be diligent—obsessive, even—in patrolling the path between the cemetery and Eden's Edge.

"I don't know about those two," Marie called out. "Someone gotta wrangle them while we got outsiders."

She was trodding down the dirt road with two large grocery sacks in her hands, stomping and grumbling. She reached me and dumped the bags at my feet.

"Ursula and Aamon?" I said. "They looked okay at Mary's funeral."

Not that I truly noticed how they were. I had been too busy straddling the veil.

"I had her hopped up on weed and Valerian root," Marie said. "And him, well, he's a conundrum."

"Naughty?" I asked.

"Not quite," Marie said, her face wrinkled in consternation. 'There's something … the fact that I don't know pisses me off."

If Marie, a seasoned witch, couldn't make sense of Aamon, I didn't have a hope in hell.

"Where are they now?" I asked.

"Locked in my cabin," she said, hooking a finger over her shoulder.

"Marie," I said. "You can't lock people up."

"And yet, I did," she said with a satisfied smirk.

I sighed. "I'll go see to them."

"You do that," she said.

Marie picked up the grocery bags and started to walk toward Kendra's hut and the campfire, but she stopped.

"Anna?" she said. "I'm not sure they belong here."

"I'm quite sure they do," I said.

"We aren't the Island of Misfit toys," Marie said. "Think of your safety, of Liza, of …"

The baby.

Yeah. There was even more to worry about now.

"They're here for a reason," I said.

"Yep," Marie agreed. "A junkie saw a free ride. Word gets around. That's it and nothing more."

Could be some truth to that. Ursula wasn't the first addict I'd taken in.

"Aamon is the key," I said. "He's supposed to be here."

Marie took a step closer to me so she could whisper. "Or perhaps he's not. Perhaps he's the worst thing that could be here, and that's why he's come."

With that, she scurried away with her bags of hot dogs and s'mores ingredients for the new arrivals. I strolled toward Ursula's cabin, my mind wandering over Eden's Edge, through the trees, and to the cemetery. I was lost in my thoughts until my shoe squished into something warm and wet.

A dead frog.

I took a step back and slipped on a stack of them.

Frogs piled four high in little cairns that peppered the walking path. There had to be hundreds of these piles of bloated frog meat oozing ichor and leaking gasses as they settled. I stepped around the dead frogs, taking care not to slip on them, but I still knocked a few cairns over with my heels, splaying them over the walking path. I wondered if I was the only one who could see them, or if they should be cleaned up before the outsiders took a stroll.

As if in answer to my thoughts, Old Friend galloped out of her home, her wild hair a birch broom in the fits, and started slurping up the frogs. Sometimes she was able to down an entire pile in one suck and gulp.

"Okay," I said, and left her to it.

I used my skeleton key to get into Ursula's cabin. Marie had cabin keys as well, but Eden's Edge was mine. I needed access to all the things, all the time. I did wonder, though, if this was the safest idea.

The image of Mary's body spilled out of her wheelchair on the lawn flashed in my mind.

Rotten bitch.

"Shut the fuck up," I scolded the voice in my head. My father's voice. Khuya.

"What?" Ursula said.

She was sitting on her couch in threadbare panties and a stained sports bra, looking as if I'd just slapped her across the face.

"Sorry, not you," I said.

She craned her neck to look over my shoulder.

"No one there, either," I said. "Just me, myself, and I."

And anyone else who resided within me.

"What are you up to?" I asked. "Where's Aamon?"

The sound of his name made her flinch. I noticed bite marks over her arms. They had always been there, but now I took note of their size. It was difficult to tell if they were from her mouth, or small enough to be from his, or if his mouth was that much smaller than hers. Only way to know was to ask.

"Has Aamon been biting you?" I asked.

Ursula looked at her arms, then bit her lip to stop it from trembling.

"Does he hurt you, Ursula?"

She shook her head but wouldn't look at me.

This could be so many things. An abusive little boy was not out of the question. Mental health concerns, sensory issues, anger deregulations. Though a demon wasn't out of the question, either.

"Well," I said, "we have other guests for the weekend. For a few nights. I'd like you to come out and mingle."

Ursula's head shaking grew more exaggerated.

"Terrible idea," she said.

"Yep," I agreed, "but it's happening. They're here. You can't hole up in here if you want to get healthy, and frankly, I don't care if you make a scene."

"What about Aamon?" she asked.

"There are children," I said. "It's important he socialize, too. He can play with them, and Kendra is running Evil Embers tonight. She's reading ghosts stories around the fire. Family friendly, I promise."

Ursula's lip bled from where her teeth had pierced the thin skin. I sat beside her on the couch, taking care to leave a buffer of space between us so she wouldn't cringe from my touch.

"Be as you are," I said. "Let the world adjust."

I'd worry about the little biting demon.

"I …" tears were falling down her face now and she

sniffled. "Okay."

The agreement came on the release of air, her tension and anxiety whooshing away in a wave of emotion.

"It's okay to be scared and uncomfortable," I said. "You have to do that first, before the comfort and happiness comes."

I left Ursula to have a cleansing cry on the couch as I went to fetch Aamon. I took gentle steps down the hardwood hallway of the cabin. I didn't want to sneak up on Aamon, but I was curious about what he did when no eyes were upon him.

I reached his door and shoved it open with my foot. It was full daylight outside, but a thick flannel blanket was pinned over the window. It was too dark to see, so I had to flick on the light. Aamon's bed was rumpled but empty, and there was a bucket on the floor beside the footboard. I peeked in the bucket even though the stench told me what it contained. Vomit, bile, urine, feces. The sheets were smeared with a mixture of all of it, and there were puddles on the floor.

Ursula had been sleeping here. This room was the fingerprint of an addict. I shut the door to bar in the odour and continued to the master bedroom. That door was open, and the room was full of sun. And from inside I could hear a crunching sound, brittle yet wet. Chewing.

Aamon was sitting cross-legged on the floor, his back to the door. His dark hair was sleek, and too black, with a sheen of purple and blue. It lay on his head in sheets, strips, no ... feathers. Ruffling like black oil slicks in the beam of sun through the dusty window. His head was rounded, his ears missing beneath the sleek dome of feathers, and his skull moved as he chewed.

"What are you eating?" I asked.

Aamon turned to me. His beak was long and hooked, and it was full of canines that dripped globs of fatty meat. I blinked, and he was a boy again—no feathers of hair, no beak, no beady eyes. His teeth were little and dull, but they were dripping carnage.

"Eatin' frogs," he said.

"Oh," I said. "Okay. Are they tasty?"

"No," he mumbled through a mouthful of frog. "They taste healthy."

"Healthy?" I asked.

Aamon swallowed, gagging down a too-large piece of frog meat, then wiped his mouth with the back of his hand. It didn't serve to clear his mouth. It only spread the gore over his pale cheeks.

Yeah," he said. "Places that gots lots of frogs are healthy. Good water, lots of plants and shit. Healthy."

"And you don't like healthy?" I asked.

Aamon plunged his hands into his pants and started massaging himself.

"I like it sick," he growled, his voice a bitonal medley of gravel voices.

"You can't shock me," I said.

He could, but I wouldn't let him know.

"You are demon," he said.

"I am witch," I replied.

From the doorway, Lavo started singing.

"Halfbreed, tainted rotten bitch."

"Listen," I said. "This is really cute, but we have outsiders here. Act right and have some fun. There will be other kids besides fucking ghosts. Play. And be good."

"Or else what?" Aamon said.

I flexed my hand and my talons pierced through my knuckles, ever so slightly. Aamon's smile gleamed and his eyes twinkled.

I thought of those campers, of the rot in the woods, of the ghosts and people all mingling, unbeknownst to each other.

"Or you won't be staying with us any longer," I said.

"If that's what you choose," Aamon and Lavo said in

unison.

I debated lopping his head off right then and there, but curiosity restrained me. Our time together wasn't done, and I was fearful of what I would find at the end.

"I'll be here at dusk to get you and your mother," I told him. Then to Lavo, "come if you want."

I shut the door behind me when I left so Ursula wouldn't have to hear her son consuming another hundred amphibians.

Chapter Twenty-One

The day was careening toward nightfall, and I wanted to ensure that everyone was in their places before we were illuminated by the moonlight, in the hour when all the darker things came out to play. Marie had all the food laid out on picnic tables—graham crackers, marshmallows, chocolate, buns and condiments. The grill was smoking with the steam and heat of dozens of hot dogs. Merle was pacing a trench at the edge of the woods, his head on a swivel between the path to the cemetery and the open landscape of Eden's Edge.

Old Friend accompanied me to retrieve Ursula and Aamon. When I walked through the door, Aamon was dressed in his Sunday best. He had on a button-down shirt tucked into khaki shorts, a sweater vest, and a little lavender bowtie. His black hair was parted to the side and carefully shaved into a gentleman's cut. And there was minimal gore on his cheeks. Not zero, but less.

"Gotta quit eating frogs, my dude," I said.

"You're not the boss of me," he snarked in that split voice of his.

"Fair enough," I said with a shrug.

Ursula was a different story. She was laid out on the couch completely naked, rubbing her clit. Her skin was covered in a sheen of sweat and blood trickled from the crook of her arm.

"For fuck's sake," I said. "Where'd she get the drugs?"

"I keep some in my butthole for her," Aamon said. "I like her better when she's high."

Ursula's hand flicked faster, harder. I left her to finish and went to her bedroom to gather some clothes. She'd be much better off with a good, solid release, though depending on what she shot up, she may get aroused again within the hour. I also grabbed a blanket to throw overtop of her if the mood to masturbate struck when she was sitting around with the campers. Might be a bit much for the outsiders to stomach, especially those with the kiddos.

Once I got Ursula cleaned up and dressed, I helped her outside, Aamon trailing behind us. We stopped twice as we walked to the woods so she could puke in the bushes. Once we reached the fork in the path, I turned away from the sound of the crackling campfire.

"Where are we going?" Aamon asked. "Isn't the party that way?"

"It isn't a party," I said, "But yes, it is. We need to make a pit stop."

"Make it yourself," he said.

I ignored him. He was beginning to feel like no more threat than a fly to an elephant.

Kendra's hut was buried just deep enough in the woods that it couldn't be seen from the open area of Eden's Edge. It was a giant mushroom, soft and rotting, with a ramshackle pair of swinging doors made from moose antlers.

"Kendra!" I called out.

I dropped Ursula in a pile of soft leaves by the door, and Aamon sat nearby on the steaming corpse of a freshly killed caribou.

"DINNAH FUCKING PUT YER ASS ON THAT!" Kendra bellowed from within the hut.

What came bursting out of those swinging doors was equal parts erotic and monstrous. A feminine creature, with supple breasts and breathtaking curves. She would be a real catch if it wasn't for her skin, which was sewn-together hides of all manner of roadkill—foxes, squirrels, deer; even a black bear. And Kendra had constructed herself a velvety pussy and perky nipples from the soft pink of a beaver's intestines.

"The fuck are you lookin at?" she growled at me.

"Hey, Kendra," I said. "This is Ursula and Aamon."

"DON'T LIKE THEM," she spat, then lifted a leg and farted at them. The air from her contracted rectum fluttered the loose rodent skin sewn onto her buttocks, causing a slapping sound that made Aamon giggle.

"They're coming to Evil Embers tonight," I explained.

"I'LL PISS ON THEM," Kendra squawked.

"Okay, be that as it may, let's keep the stories light," I said, then I pointed at Aamon. "I don't want *that* getting any more riled than he is."

"Hey!" Aamon said, feigning offense.

"And some of the campers have children with them," I said.

Kendra sniffed the air and hobbled over to the carcass where Aamon was sitting. She sniffed him, then her tongue snaked out and penetrated his ear. He swatted at her face and tumbled back off the caribou, but not before Kendra got a good scoop of his ear wax on her tongue. She rolled it around her mouth, swallowed it, then belched.

"Huh," she said. "What is you?"

"Yo Momma!" he yelled. He rubbed his elbow where he had banged it on a rock in his fall. His eyes were wet with little kid tears, which gave me pause.

Just a child.

"You gots yourself a twig and berries," Kendra said, pointing a twisted finger at Aamon's crotch, "so you ain't yo momma, unless she birthed you from her bowels. Which is entirely possible, from the look of ye."

"Fuck you," Aamon said.

"So, you see what I'm saying," I said to Kendra.

"Uh huh," she agreed. "Keep it cool with my stories, indeed the coldest. Real tight and quiet."

Kendra studied the lad for a solid minute while he shifted uncomfortably under the gaze of her hazy grey eyes. She finally broke away and disappeared back into her house, grumbling and farting as she rooted around inside with a great deal of crashing, smashing, and splintering of wood.

"Don't worry," I said to Ursula and Aamon. "That's just her way."

We started back toward Eden's Edge.

"What is she?" Aamon asked.

"Ghoul," I said. "Not really dead. I picked her up from …"

I didn't want to tell Aamon about the cemetery. I wasn't sure if he knew about it already, but it felt like a bad idea to make him aware. "I picked her up in the woods. She was eating bodies off the ground. I gave her a place to stay in exchange for her helping Merle with the upkeep of the grounds and woods."

"Like a crypt keeper!" Aamon said.

"Sort of?" I said. "But this particular ghoul, in life, had an affinity for books. She's a veritable mental library of all that is fictional and historical. You don't need books with Kendra around."

Kendra would have replaced her entire fungus hut with a full library if her skin didn't turn everything paper to mush and mold. She had to read books fast; they all turned to liquid within hours of her touch. Thankfully, in her living years, she'd consumed ten lifetimes worth of books.

Aamon didn't ask anymore questions, and Ursula was floating along on another plane, so the walk out of the woods was quiet, save for a low rumble off in the distance. My eyes found the skies peeking through the tree branches, but I spied no storms. The rumble was constant, unlike thunder, but I couldn't quite hear it. It was a sound beneath all others, a baritone whisper of a pulse. I tried to focus on the birdsong, on the chirps of frogs emerging from their burrows for the night, on the creaking of the branches in the evening breeze. But though it was quieter than all of that, the foreign white noise persisted, drawing my attention. I scanned the trees, the darkening paths, even Aamon and Ursula, who carried on like nothing was awry.

The sound got no louder or softer when we stepped out of the woods into the clearing that was Eden's Edge. The campfire area was bustling with activity as the new campers mingled about and Marie worked away at starting the fire. The ghost children had gathered around, always anxious to hear Kendra's tales.

Dusk was heavy, leaning into night, and it was difficult to see across the expanse of Eden's Edge. But I did see the door to Old Friend's house open and its occupants spill onto the path out front.

First, it was the New Friends. Dozens upon dozens of little girls, all wearing different outfits, none with heads. Some looked wealthy, some wore tattered rags, some barefoot, others in fancy black patent shoes. They marched single file down the front step, toward the trees, then along the perimeter of the forest. A whole cacophony of Friends followed, all with arachnid legs and contorted bodies, heads full of stringy hair. They, too, formed the marching line that continued to snake around the perimeter. Old Friends came last, shuffling out of the house on aching feet and brittle bones, skin sagging like melted wax, teeth missing, eyes rheumy, breasts long. Soon, all of Eden's Edge was surrounded by a perimeter of Friends—New, Mid, and Old. They became absolutely still and silent; sentries that blended into the forest.

Lavo met us as we came out of the forest, and she and Aamon ran off toward the bonfire. Marie had the fire blazing with crackles, snaps, and orange flames that licked up at the stars. The campers had brought chairs around and were sipping on red solo cups full of libations and lip looseners. I hoped that they'd cross the line of intoxication before Kendra came out to start her stories. She might be more palatable that way.

I guided Ursula to a hammock chair and draped the blanket over her. She was smiling and muttering to herself while flames danced in her eyes. She seemed happy and comfortable enough, and quiet for the moment. I gazed up at the trees and gave Erinyes a nod. Taking my cue, the ruby bird fluttered down and perched on the back of the chair to supervise Ursula while I checked on the other activities.

"Meat's good!" Marie said as I approached the covered area.

She'd loaded up a dozen sticks with hot dogs to be roasted over the fire. There was a tray of s'mores ingredients ready for once dinner was over and the stories had begun.

"How is everyone getting on?" I asked.

"Well, the lads are madly in love," Marie said as she nodded to a couple cuddled up together in a set of double camping chairs. "They can barely keep their tongues out of each other's throats. The woman has been quiet, mostly watching everyone else, and the teens have been tossing leaves and flowers into the fire."

The last of the campers, the family of four, were still under the awning of their RV. The mom was in a rocking chair nursing an infant, and the dad was helping a little boy pump up the tire of his bicycle. I wandered over to them; the boy noticed me first and gave a tentative wave.

"Hello," I said and returned his wave. "I'm Anna."

"Oh, hi!" the dad said. He stood and wiped his hands on his pants, then extended me a handshake. "The owner, yes?"

I nodded. "Are you settling in okay? Have everything you need?"

"And them some," he said. "Traveling with kiddos is never light."

I smiled. I couldn't relate. I never had a family, and when I travelled by myself, it was mostly with only the clothes on my back.

"Camping with a baby is something else," the mom said as she switched the infant from breast to breast. "We never traveled with him," she said, motioning to the boy who was now on his bike and riding in circles around the RV. "Thought we better start now that we have her."

The woman's daughter gurgled on her nipple, and milk bubbled at her lips.

"Life goes by too fast," the mom said. "We don't want to miss out while we are just going through the motions. We gotta do more than just survive."

I stared at her, and she stared at me. It was like she was talking to me, or was me, and my head buzzed, my hearts pounded.

"Story time!" Marie called, breaking the trance.

"You go on," the mom said to her husband and little boy. "I'll head over when she's finished eating."

The dad took his little boy by the hand and walked him toward the campfire. The mom was smiling at them, no longer paying attention to me.

I was getting paranoid.

"Let me know if you need anything," I said.

"Will do!" she said with a smile.

It was Liza's smile on that woman's face. And suddenly, Liza's hair and black eyes, with an infant suckling her dark nipple.

"Anna?"

"Yes, Kaz," I said, turning away from the mom who was herself again, no trace of Liza.

"Want me to keep an eye on things here?" he asked. "Merle's gone to the cemetery."

Troubling. I wondered what was going on back there. Why Merle would leave.

"Yes please," I said. "Mainly keep an eye on Ursula and Aamon, if you don't mind."

"Will do," he said. "But …"

Kaz's eyes drifted to the woods, to the path Merle would have walked. Kaz was no stranger to demons. His coworker had been one and had taken his life away once he realized it.

"If I need you for that," I said, motioning in the cemetery, "I'll call for you."

"Lots of demons, Merle told me," he said.

"Lots of something that doesn't belong on our side," I said.

"I'll stay alert," he said.

Of that, I had no doubt. Kaz was always a cop, always out to protect.

Everyone was gathered around the fire when I reached it, bundled in blankets and munching on the food. Marie had the people arranged into a U shape around the fire, leaving an open space for Kendra to tell her stories. Merle had dropped a large log for Kendra to stand on, though Kendra often preferred to pace while speaking. Helped her to think, she said.

The sun had fully dipped below not only the trees but the horizon, leaving Eden's Edge in an oppressive darkness only alleviated by the flames of the campfire. Marie had let it die down a touch so people could see each other, and Kendra, over the flames.

"Here she comes," Marie said.

I'd have much preferred the flames were higher. Seeing

Kendra was not something everyone could stomach.

The branches creaked and strained as Kendra appeared from the woods. To maintain the charade of being a human, Kendra donned a large cloak made of two caribou hides stitched together with fishing twine and a mask cut from a beaver pelt. The children gasped as she approached the fire.

"Cool costume!" the boy said.

"Hot as Bayou pussy," Kendra growled beneath her mask.

"For fuck's sake," I said under my breath.

"Kendra!" Marie scolded.

"Better than my skins, I suppose," Kendra said, referring to the patchwork false skin she'd used to cover the decay of her ghoulish form.

"Everyone," Marie said. "This is Kendra, our storyteller. Now who likes spooky stories?"

The children and the adults clapped and cheered.

"But not too spooky," I cautioned, glaring into the eyeholes cut into Kendra's beaver hide.

Kendra answered with a fart and a grunt. She dragged her hides and her own carcass up to the opening in the circle and spread her arms wide.

"Welcome," she said, "to Eden's Edge. And Welcome to Evil Embers, a night of tales and terrors."

Kendra's head tilted toward me and she froze. What was she looking at? I checked my body, ensuring my rot was not showing, but there was nothing that wasn't covered up by sweats and a hoodie. Everyone was looking now, and I realized they weren't looking at me when Liza slid her hand into mine.

"What are you doing here?" I asked.

"Needed to get out of the house," she said.

She was panting, and her other hand pressed into the small of her back. She was huge, her belly distended, hiking up her shirt. If I'd seen her on the street, I would have guessed she was 11 months pregnant with quadruplets.

"You need to sit," I said.

Marie was already on it. She hauled over an adirondack chair and backed it up to Liza so all she had to do was fall back into it. Getting her out of it would be a challenge, but we'd deal with that later.

I sat in the dirt beside Liza, her hand still in mine, and looked over the fire at Kendra. Kendra's head was tilted and her body quite still.

"Oh, looky here," she cooed. "Methinks I'll have a change of plans, another story I'd like to tell."

I gave her a hard look. A warning. Kendra tented her fingers and let out a hearty chortle.

"Shall we begin?" she said.

Chapter Twenty-Two

"Welcome to Evil Embers, cunts!

"You're all going to listen to my tale and you're gonna love it, love it you are.

"I was going to tell you a tale about a porridge thieving whore, or about a bitch using a wig as a rope ladder, but I sees a special guest in the crowd tonight, and I'm inspired to weave a different yarn.

"So here we go. Plunk your asses on stumps or in chairs, shove your mouths full of meats and sweets, and let me paint a picture for ye.

"Once upon a time, the bible was shit. Ain't no god be weaving trees and beasts. The earth and the stars formed, a collision of dirt and sparkles and everything between. The stars were cold and full of fire, raging with violence and horny for power. They were big, the stars; unmatched, glittering beautiful like titties. Gossamer, ethereal, and radiant.

"The dirt was warm, feral, intimate and full of life. Birth, healing, peace. Pitch, thick and heady.

"The stars and the dirt, gossamer and pitch, threw different beings like pottery, crafting and carving until they each had their own. Beasts awoke, both great and small, weak and strong, smart and stupid.

"The dichotomy could not exist together. *Should* not. Gossamer and pitch were too much in conflict. Thus came the veil.

"The dirt was possible, attainable, reachable. You could feel the dirt, use it, be it. Humans, plants, animals. Feather and flesh, scale and tail, root and bone. The possible. And those who lead and maintained the order, with the magic of nature in their blood. Witches. Our matriarchs. Mother.

"The beasts of the stars were untouchable, foreign to creatures of the flesh, destructive and horrific. Ghosts, ghouls, demons, specters. The impossible. Destructors intent on penetration, of seeping through to control what does not belong to them. The patriarch. Father.

"Mostly, the matriarch haunts the earth, the patriarch, the stars.

"But occasionally, stardust glitters the soil, and the veil swishes to the side, parts like pussy lips to invite in the beast. Chaos and confusion ripple the gossamer, disperses the fog, and throws all into chaos.

"Murder, mayhem, ghosts, cannibals, zombies, murderers, vampires, cryptids, rapists, demons.

"Hate, blood, pain.

"Not oft the two shall meet. And when they do, all is set wrong. Gossamer wrapped 'round stardust, penetrating the moist pitch of the welcoming earth. A violent, passionate fucking that spurts out a mess of a babe that leaves horror and destruction in her wake, because she is horror, she is destruction, she was never possible, never impossible, never meant to be, she was

"Fog and steam,

Gossamer and Pitch ..."

Chapter Twenty-Three

"Half-breed tainted rotten bitch," I said, my voice a whisper.

Everyone around the fire heard me. Guess I hadn't been that quiet after all. They stared at me as the wood crackled, and the flame licked at the night sky.

"Don't make no sense," Aamon said, his lip in a pout. "This story is stupid."

Kendra hissed, her forked tongue snapping out from beneath her hood.

"*You're* fucking stupid," she spat at Aamon.

"Am not!" he cried.

My head was humming, spinning. The Friends surrounding the perimeter of Eden's Edge were swaying like trees, humming to match the tone in my mind. Or create it.

"It's gibberish," Aamon said. "Like some stupid poetry."

"Prophecy?" I said, trying to figure it out for myself.

"NOT!" Kendra squealed, her voice a pig's bray. "Neither poetry nor prophecy. It just is."

"Is what?" I asked.

Kendra hobbled over to me, leaning on a giant tree branch Merle had fashioned into a crutch for her. When she reached me, she spoke the words directly into my mouth.

"Naught more than a mistake," she said. "Turnt sperm deviled the egg that made ye."

The laugh that roared out of Kendra startled everyone around the fire. Jaws were slack, and the infant began to cry.

"Dumb," Aamon said. "All those words and no story."

Kendra's head snapped toward him.

"Ye's just thick, is all," Kendra said, sweeping a skeletal finger at Aamon, then around the crowd. "The lot of ye. Daft as a crop o' turnip."

"Then what's the point?" Aamon said. "What's it about?"

"I told ye!" Kendra's voice was crescendoing. She loved her books, her tales, and when people didn't share in that love, or understand her stories, she became feral.

I should have calmed her down. Should have guided her away and given her a moment to compose herself. Marie could have told stories instead, some recycled fairytale bullshit, standard-issue, comfortable and familiar. But I was frozen, Kendra's tale rattling around my skull.

"What does it mean, then?" Aamon said. "I think you're just a dumb old hag with all-timers."

Oh no.

One thing people could never do was question Kendra's mental faculties.

She stalked up to Aamon, grabbed him by the collar, and hoisted him off the ground until his face was inside her hood.

I didn't expect what came next.

Kendra jabbed a finger toward me, pointing, accusing.

"The story's about her mere and pere," Kendra said. "A

witch and a demon fucked, and his seed slurped into her egg, and BOOM. We get this mistake. This half-breed rotten bitch who can't make heads nor tails of her magic or destruction."

I was powerless to move, to respond, to react. And Kendra kept on her roll.

"And now, because of the war within her, she's wreaking a path of havoc through her life, and all the lives adjacent to hers. Finger and claws from both sides of the veil are reaching for her, trying to claim her, but those teeth and nails are finding purchase on everything but her."

Aamon writhed and squirmed, trying to free himself of Kendra's grasp.

"And you," she hissed. "Little spawn. You want it to continue. To let it happen, let this chaos continue until all that's left is pain and ash."

An arm around my waist. My feet lift off the ground, but only a few centimeters. Merle was slowly carrying me off into the woods.

The campers didn't know where to look. They were transfixed by Kendra's rant, but also glancing at me, wondering what it all meant, even though I had no clue what the fuck was happening. What had been happening my entire life? It was all falling apart and coming together at the same time.

Marie grabbed Kendra by the elbow.

"Time to go," Marie said as she spun the ghoul around.

Kendra dropped Aamon on his head. He cursed and spat at her, then scurried off to his mother's side.

Marie was not very big or spry, so she'd have never been able to move Kendra by herself. Thankfully, Kaz was there, doing most of the heavy work, wrangling Kendra away from her audience. I hope that it appeared, to the guests, that Marie was ushering her off, though. I couldn't explain that story, nor could I explain ghosts, ghouls, or witches.

Marie and Kaz handed Kendra off to me and Merle, then Marie scurried back to the fire. I could hear her placating the uneasy crowd.

"Now then," Marie said. "How about a real story! This one is better for the kids. It's called Woom …"

"Gahhhh!" Merle was scolding Kendra as he pulled her deeper into the woods.

"I don't care none about them fucking little crotch fruits!" Kendra snapped. "I'll be using whatever language I please 'round them!"

"Gahhhh!" Merle bellowed, and he gave Kendra a solid cuff upside the head.

The flesh mask Kendra had fashioned as a face spun around backward, and she lashed out toward Merle. Because she couldn't see, she raked her nails into a tree, instead.

"Fuck you, you bloody reaven, lopsided rotten piece of shit!"

"GAHHHH!"

Merle tackled Kendra to the forest floor, and they rolled around, ripping at each other, strips of Kendra's skin suit tearing away, revealing the rotting mass of grey goo and bones beneath.

I didn't need to stay and supervise. They were both dead—well, undead—so they could fuss around like feral toddlers all they wished. I walked deeper into the woods, my mind racing.

Was I not meant to be?

So what? I am. I exist.

But at what cost?

The cemetery suddenly appeared before me like I hadn't journeyed far at all. Fog had settled in, covering the headstones like gossamer. The lychgate was tilted and sealed, as I'd left it, but rot had consumed the grounds regardless. The earth was spoiled, the grass gone, replaced by dark fungus that oozed pus and steam.

I closed my eyes and the world turned green. A memory. Liza, me, Mary, and Laz, playing in the cemetery as kids.

New Friend was there, laid out on a grave, the sun warming her grey skin.

I wished to go back to that moment. Live in it for a spell, maybe never come out. Would it have been so bad if it had all ended that day? Liza, Mary, and Laz would never have had Bobby inside of them, would have never had their blood spilled and spirits broken. How different would we all have been? Would Liza and I have still ended up together? Would Mary and Laz have kiddos of their own? Would we all still be alive? Would we be happy?

Life was careening by too fast. A second chance at happiness was sifting through my fingers like find sand. Time was running out.

I wish I'd chosen differently. I wish I'd been different. I wish I'd embraced who I was a lot sooner, soon enough to save everyone. Mom, Mary, Laz.

Liza.

The trees behind me rustled. A branch snapped.

I turned to see. All the Friends that had been lining the perimeter of Eden's Edge were there, standing in a row, watching. The line snaked back through the forest, far as I could see.

"What do I do?" I asked them.

A cry belched out from the cemetery. I closed my eyes again. New Friend was laid out prone on the grass, and hands burst through the plot below, wrapping around her and trying to pull her down into the earth.

This had happened before. When I was a child. Someone, or someones, trying to drag New Friend down into the earth.

'What do I do?" I screamed.

I scrambled across the slick black fungus to the spot in my memory where New Friend lay. I clawed at the dirt, digging it to the side like a dog. I was frantic, panicked, dirt and grimy mold flying everywhere, going inside me, coating my eyes. I stopped when my fingers penetrated flesh, releasing a waft of gasses and decay that cause my stomach to heave. I wiped my eyes with filthy hands, smearing away enough muck to see what I had found beneath the soil.

An abdomen, small and pale, blotched with bloat and death. I continued to excavate, more precise and gentle this time, until New Friend's body was completely exposed. She was naked, headless, and rotting. One hand was placed over her heart, the other laced through something in the dirt.

Another hand.

I continued to dig, uncover, wipe away dirt. New Friend was holding Friend's hand, and Friend was holding Old Friend's hand. They were buried all in a row, all naked and bloated and blue, exactly the versions I'd known in my life, except very dead now.

What would New Friend have looked like, had she had a head?

What would Friend have been like if the taint of my father's blood had not elongated and contorted her limbs?

What would Old Friend have been like, had life not sucked her dry of all hope?

The hand New Friend held over her heart suddenly shot up and grabbed me by the throat. Old Friend's free hand lurched up as well, grabbing me by the face and pulling me on top of Friend. I tried to fight, clawing skin and biting at fingers, but it was three against one. We folded in on each other, and soon I couldn't breathe. I was compressed between them with mouthfuls of dirt spilling into my lungs. They squeezed so hard that we pressed into each other, my head rolling off my shoulders and settling on New Friend's body. Old Friend's folds of loose skin absorbed me, and Friend's sharp, jagged bones pierced through me and clanked against my own skeleton.

We were one, and we were dying. An undulated pile of rot in the ground.

"Save them."

I coughed, and a great glob of dirt soaked in mucous and blood spewed from my throat. I gulped in air and opened my eyes. I was at the bottom of a grave again, looking up the dark tunnel of my dig to the coffin-shaped hole framing the night sky. And there was Lavo, her silhouette peering down at me.

"You look like a flower," she said. "Did someone plant you?"

I struggled to my feet at the bottom of the grave.

"You're naked," Aamon said. "I see you boobies and your front butt."

I *was* naked. And these kids were watching me, their two little heads dark orbs at the opening of my grave.

"Help me out," I said, reaching my hand up.

The kids spoke in unison, a harmonic duet. But where Lavo was smiling, her tune chipper, Aamon's eyes were wide with horror, his face drawn into a grimace.

"They're all dying," they said, her, ecstatic, him, horrified.

Behind them, somewhere far away, a baby cried.

"Stay here," Lavo said. "It's beautiful down there."

"No!" Aamon said, and he struck Lavo with a right hook.

Lavo laughed as they fought, their heads now out of view.

"Fuck," I said as I tried to crawl out of the grave with little success. The children were fighting out of sight, their sounds of snapping, snarling, and giggling echoing through the woods. The more I tried to climb out, the more dirt collapsed into the grave. I clawed faster, trying to build a dirt pile to stand on, but the dirt was loose and thin, and compressed under my weight. I was winded, and everything hurt, and I was about to give up when a massive pale hand reached down from the sky.

"Gahhhh."

Merle grabbed my hand and hauled me out of my grave.

"Merle, what's happening?"

He wasn't looking at me. He was looking at the edge of the cemetery. There sat a wolf with a serpent's tail, Lavo swinging from its massive jaws.

"Save them," she said from her dead mouth. "Get back in the dirt. Save me."

In the distance, a baby wailed.

The crowd was crawling with dermisted beetles, consuming everything they touched.

"Let them cleanse," Lavo said.

"They are dying!" Aamon shouted through his wolf snout.

I ran, and Merle passed me, leading the way to Eden's Edge. I followed the loping of his single yellow boot as we ducked and dodged tree branches and detritus that had been thrown in our path. The line of Friends ran, too, alongside us deep in the trees. Behind us, the lychgate groaned, and the sound of it cracking was like a whip. The music of hell thundered behind us—hooves, footsteps, claws, sliding, squelching bodies. All hell was spilling out around me, but I knew I had to get back. I had to save them, and this was the way.

Chapter Twenty-Four

I smelled the carnage before I saw it.

"I don't know, I don't know, I don't know," Marie chanted as she paced to and fro around the glowing embers of the campfire. She swatted at a pile of dermisted beetles that were congregating on the trays of food.

Miss Mojo was there, too, but as a business of blue bottle flies rather than the plump, joyful woman who'd hold me to her bosom and tell me everything was going to be okay. She couldn't help but be these flies, I was sure. The stench of feces and urine was thick in the air, and her flies were ravenous to dip their feet and feelers in the waste.

Kaz was crying dry tears as he went from body to body, attempting to feel for pulses, but his fingers dissipated like fog whenever he touched solid flesh.

They were all dead. All of them. The couples, the solo camper, the children. And they had not died quiet deaths. The bonfire area was coated in dark brown vomit, and the campers' clothes were soiled with all bodily fluids possible. Their eyes were open, and capillaries as thick as worms and red as blood marred the whites.

"Poison," I said.

I looked at Marie, at the trays of hotdogs and S'mores. I ran over and licked pieces of the food. There was a slight floral tang to everything, and a mild, powdery texture.

"Aqua Tofana, with hints of nightshade and lavender," Lavo said. "It's been a proven recipe for me throughout time."

Lavo strolled out of the woods, a wolf's head dangling from her grasp.

"What the fuck did you do?" I asked.

"You keep holding on, even though your life is broken," she said. "You need to let go. Save them. I'm cleansing so you can move on."

The wolf's tongue lolled out of its mouth, dragging through the dirt. Black chunks mottled the mange around its lips. Lavo had poisoned it, too. Poisoned Aamon, whatever he was.

"It's just a head," she said with a shrug, and she rolled it across the ground where it settled at Marie's feet. "He's got many."

"Beast!" Marie screamed.

She stopped pacing and focused her attention on the wolf's head and Lavo.

"You meanie!" Aamon screeched.

There was another Aamon, this one with blue flesh and black eyes. He rose from where he'd been draped over Ursula. She was crumpled on the ground, limbs twitching, eyes rolled into the back of her head. He lunged for Lavo but she was quick, sidestepping him with ease.

Kaz hesitated between the children and the bodies, neither of which he'd be able to help. I motioned to Ursula, and Kaz came to me as I rolled her on her side. Ursula vomited a slurry of black and yellow curds into the grass.

"Ursula, what did you take?" I asked.

"Probably the goddamn hotdogs!" Marie shrieked. "How did I not notice they were poisoned?"

"Because you weren't meant to," I said.

"Demons," she hissed at the children.

I wasn't so sure. Aamon was, but Lavo …

"No … blood," Ursula gasped.

"Water," I said to Marie.

"Not a fucking chance," Marie said. "Everything could be laced with the poison."

Ursula screamed and clutched her belly, then purged another violent stream of vomit toward the fire.

"Get water from your house then," I said. "Safer than moving her."

Marie hustled off to get water, and I stroked Ursula's hair to calm her. Just like Merle did for me so many times, just like Mom used to.

"About time to die," Ursula said, her voice strained from the pain.

"Did you try to kill yourself?" I said to Ursula.

She nodded.

"Did you poison the food?"

She shook her head.

"Was it Aamon? Lavo?"

She shrugged, and another swell of pain wracked her body, curling her into a ball.

"What did you take?" I asked once her muscles relaxed.

Ursula let her arm go slack and flop in the dirt, revealing several fresh track marks.

Heroin.

"That it?" I asked.

She reached into the pouch of her hoodie and tossed out several empty pill bottles. The motion made her sick again, and she vomited up chunks of chewed hotdogs.

"Ah," I said with a sigh. "The poison, too."

I wasn't sure she could be saved. I certainly couldn't save her myself, though I half considered forcing dirt through her veins and organs to neutralize the toxins.

"You have a child, Ursula," I said. "Aamon."

I could never imagine willingly leaving my own child, even if he was a demon.

"No … blood," she repeated.

Her voice was wet, her breathing strained and shallow. She didn't have long left.

"What do you mean?" I asked. "He has no blood?"

Ursula reached for my hand and pressed it against her abdomen.

"No blood," she said, and she started to laugh.

I searched for a scar, a mark, something; but there was nothing.

"Endometrial ablation," Ursula said.

I stopped. Thought.

"Doc wouldn't give me a hysterectomy, even though I asked," she said. "He said I was too young and might want kids one day. Like a fuck up like me should be in charge of other humans."

She laughed and cried all at once, vomit dribbling out of her nose and off her lips.

"You couldn't conceive," I said.

She patted her tummy and shook her head. "Ablated. No blood. No period, no conception."

"Where did Aamon come from?" I asked.

With great effort, Ursula rolled on her back and thrust her hands down her pants, laughing maniacally as she shoved a fist inside herself.

"I birthed him!" she cackled. "It's impossible, but I got fucked, and my belly grew, and I shat out Aamon. He was too big, never a baby, and I ripped and my bones splintered, and he fixed me right up and sent us on our way!"

Ursula was both sobbing and laughing, her body twitching in pain.

"Who, Ursula?" I asked. "Who got you pregnant? Who fixed you up?"

Like a hunted animal, Ursula scanned the trees, the fire pit, the cabins. Her eyes stopped when she focused at the top of my house, and her jaw went slack before she belted out a blood curdling scream. I tried to grab her, to hold her, but she scrambled backward, screeching and trying to get to her feet.

I looked over at my cabin. At the shadowy figure that stood on the peak, black muscles rippling in the moonlight. He had four cocks—an erect cock resting on each shoulder, one in his mouth, and the other tucked between his legs and up inside him.

Trebor. Khuya.

Dad.

Ursula's screaming stopped. I realized too late what that meant. When I turned back to her, she had a smile on her face, and an even larger smile gashed open across her throat. There was a smashed bottle of beer in her hand, dripping blood into the dirt.

She dropped dead with her eyes on Khuya.

My talons burst from my knuckles. I didn't know who I was going to slash, or what I was going to do, or if there was any imminent danger left.

Besides myself. I did this.

I was never meant to be.

In the midst of Ursula's end, I'd lost track of Lavo and Aamon; they were nowhere to be seen. In the chaos, the woods had fallen silent, but beneath the unnatural hush was a moan. A cry.

Liza.

I stood and walked toward my cabin, my eyes on my father who stood on the peak, a wicked grin cracking open his face. When I reached the door, it swung open and I was greeted by my mom.

"Anna," she said. "You are smart, you are strong, and you can do this."

Chapter Twenty-Five

The house was warm. The fire crackled in the hearth, and my mind went to past times I'd been in front of that fire—Mom and I, mugs in hand, drinking tea and reading books. Liza and I entwined, pleasure rippling through us, spurting, convulsing with ecstasy as we put a life inside her.

I didn't feel myself walking, but I moved toward the bedroom regardless, in a ghostly float. The door opened when I reached it.

Marie was at the head of the bed with herbs and tinctures. Miss Mojo was butterflies fanning Liza's skin, which was soaked in a sheen of sweat and blood. Erinyes balanced on the headboard; Gus's tail wrapped around her trembling body.

"She's in a bad way," Marie said, her eyes red and lower lip trembling.

Liza was so big. Her stomach was a mess of purple and silver stretch marks, and the mass of whatever was inside her moved and rolled, causing her to wince and groan. She was naked, her feet up in makeshift stirrups that I assumed Merle must have crafted out of moose antlers. He'd even lined them with thick red flannel to make them soft and warm for her.

"We should cut it out," I said, feeling but not hearing the words rolling off my tongue. "Save her."

Marie touched my arm. A butterfly kissed my face and landed on my shoulder.

Liza screamed, and her knees fell to the sides as she clawed at her inner thighs and labia.

She spoke, pleading. "Save—"

A gasp stole both Liza's words and her scream. Marie grabbed Liza's hand. The butterflies fanned faster, harder, stirring up a cooling breeze.

I went to Liza's side, took her hand, and put my other hand on her belly. Whatever was inside of Liza responded to my touch, pressing into my palm.

"Liza," I said.

"I love you," she said. She smiled, and a tear rolled down her cheek, soaking into her raven-black hair. "I'm ready."

"To be a mom?" I said.

She shook her head. "No," she said, quiet but sure. "For this to be over."

"For what to be over?" I asked.

"Everything," she said.

I was going to argue, to say something encouraging, but there was nothing left to say. I glanced up at the wall, at the image painted there in blood.

Three hearts squeezed together, surrounded by the totems of my life. The bird, the squirrel, the wolf.

Liza's head snapped up, and she looked to the end of the bed. Lavo was there holding one of her feet, Aamon the other. They were pulling her legs wide, so she was open to the room.

"End this," Lavo said.

"End it," Aamon said.

They were talking about two different things, but I didn't know what.

My talons had since retracted, but they emerged out of my flesh a few millimeters before Liza took my hand again. Good thing, or I would have beheaded both the little bastards.

"Save—" Liza couldn't finish before she was gripped by another contraction.

The scream that belted out of Liza shook all of Eden's Edge and the forest beyond. The woods were lit with activity, snarling and thrashing and cracking wood. Marie glanced nervously at the window as the glass shuddered, and the walls of the cabin groaned from the pressure outside.

"Her," Liza said.

I kissed her lips. She tasted like fruit and fire. My tears dripped onto her face, and she licked them away.

"Save her," Liza said.

"Her?" I asked.

Liza curled up as she gripped my fist, wracked by another contraction. She was gripping another hand too—someone standing on the other side of the bed. But Marie had moved to her feet with a basin of water and a towel.

"Mom," I said, my voice broken, my words coated in a sob.

Mom spoke, her voice a song.

"You are smart, you are strong. You are loved."

Liza's water broke in a violent gush, coating Marie and splashing to the floor. So much fluid; too much, flooding the room up to our ankles.

"Push!" Marie yelled, and Liza bore down. Mom and I squeezed her hands and Liza squeezed in return.

"Push," Miss Mojo's butterflies whispered.

Mom continued her chant, steady and true …

You are smart, you are strong, you are loved

… while Erinyes and Gus chittered and flapped above

us on the headboard.

"Please," Liza said, her eyes locked on mine.

"Save her," Lavo said.

"Kill her," Aamon said.

"Save us," Liza pleaded.

I kissed her. It tasted like it was our first kiss, our lips salty with tears, our flesh tingling and electric. Liza gasped into my mouth and went still. So very still; too quiet. I pulled back and looked into her eyes. They were wide, fixed. A single tear rolled down her cheek.

"Anna," Marie said.

The room was ripe with the stench of blood and death. Everyone was completely still; eyes trained on the bloody mass in Marie's arms.

NO!

"No!" I screamed.

Aamon laughed.

"Good," he said.

"Give her to me," I said to Marie.

No one moved. Even Erinyes's wings were still. All eyes were open, no one was blinking, no chests were rising and falling with breath.

"Give her to me!" I screamed.

I launched over the bed and grabbed my baby from Marie.

"Liza!" I cried. "Mom, help me! Mom!"

The baby was dead. Maybe it'd never been alive. She was stunning; a bundle of pale, wrinkled flesh covered in vernix and blood. I held her against my body, willed my warmth into her.

Liza was a statue on the bed, like a piece of art. A sculpture. Her head was lolled to the side, legs splayed open. I set the babe between her legs and posed her in the same position as Liza.

A beautiful baby girl, curls both black and white. One

eye glacial blue, the other, black. Pudgy, pink, perfect.

All except for the gaping chest.

Her chest was wide open, as if cracked by a surgeon, ribs pried apart to reveal her insides. Everything was accounted for—stomach and GI tract, liver, kidneys, lungs …

No heart.

I looked to my mom, who stared back into my eyes. Lavo was at her side, holding her hand. They said in unison, voices young and old,

Save her

And they smiled; a sad sight.

On the other side, my dad and Aamon, hand in hand.

Leave her be. Let her stay dead.

"How?" I asked, frantic, not sure which pair I was directing the question at.

The baby was dead. She had no heart. How could I save her? Maybe it was Liza I could save.

"Can I save *her*?" I screeched.

I left the baby between Liza's legs and hopped up on the bed, straddling Liza, and started CPR. I worked until I was breathless, sweat dripping with my tears onto Liza's breasts, my hands pumping with force until I felt Liza's ribs fracture. My hearts pounded, threatening to burst from my chest. The cracking of Liza's ribs mirrored the cracking of mine. I pivoted, looked at the baby, back at Liza. And I knew.

I slid off the bed, grabbed the baby, and ran down the hall, past the kitchen where Mom and I had shared toast and eggs our first morning in Eden's Edge, past the living room where Liza and I had made love so many times, where this baby had come to be, and out the front door.

No one was waiting for me outside. No sign of Merle or Kaz. No Friends—New, Old, or otherwise. The campers were still there, dead in piles by the bonfire as I passed. I had just about reached the woods when Aamon called out to me.

"Don't," he said, his voice deep. An adult man.

"Fuck you!" I yelled at him.

"Leave it alone," he said. "Just lay back and let it happen, the way it was meant to be. Put her in the fire."

He wanted me to do nothing. To live out my life like this, barely surviving, waiting to die. He wanted the destruction of my existence.

"It was never meant to be," Lavo said, dipping her chin to me or the baby, I'm not sure. "And this child is a second chance."

Dermisted beetles flowed from Lavo's every orifice, scattering across Eden's Edge on a mission to devour. They coated the bodies, the fire, the structures. It was impossible, how quick they worked. Faster than my fire when I'd razed Eden's Edge all those years ago.

Aamon turned to Lavo and screamed. His jaw elongated into a wolf's maw and fire spewed as he hollered. His voice was a flamethrower, as it was meant to be. As it was for Aamon, the Grand Marquis of Hell.

"You are my sister," he said to me, flames hissing from his tongue. "We need to reconcile, as a family."

Trebor walked behind Aamon, his four cocks spurting flames from their tips.

"A family of demons," I said. "You want everything to be destroyed."

YOU'VE DONE WELL, Trebor said, both to me and my brother. ..

Suppose I had. Everything and everyone around me was reduced to pain and death.

I looked at the baby in my arms; her skin beginning to bloat and fade to blue.

A sweet aroma reached my nose from the woods. Perfume and flowers. Mom.

"You want everything gone," I said, my eyes floating to Lavo, then back down to the baby. "Everything … except her."

Though they drew no breath, I saw both Trebor and Aamon's chests hitch with anticipation.

I bolted down the path to the cemetery, holding the baby close, her fractured ribs piercing my chest. The woods were buzzing with the sound of all the voices, all the lives I'd ruined, all the lives that had ruined me.

Mom
Miss Mojo
Marie
Mary
Laz
Allison
Bobby
Robbie Cum Crocs
Kaziel
Empusa
Liza. Liza. Liza. Liza.

I ran, and they all ran with me, their voices, their touch, and their scents threatening to drive me mad. The night sky swirled with a tornadic chaos of noise and lightning, beasts swooping overhead threatening to tear me apart. I tripped on a tree root and fell flat on my stomach, crushing the baby beneath me with a sickening squelch. I mewled like an injured animal and rolled on my side, curling around the baby's corpse to protect what was left, even if it was only a single hair on her precious head.

Hands tucked beneath me, lifting me up, holding me against a massive body. I was carried down the path toward the cemetery against a chest that had no heartbeat, no warmth, but all the love. I watched the ground, noting all the flowers and brush as we passed. It was all the dark indigo and grey of night, save the single flash of yellow every time Merle's boot stepped into my view.

After what seemed like years, the thick brush parted, and we stepped onto the barren waste that was the infected cemetery. Merle set me on my feet and hugged me.

"Thank you," I said.

I kissed his cheek, just above the place where his lower jaw was missing. I was sure he'd be smiling if he had a mouth.

"Gahhhh," he said.

"I love you, too," I said.

It was time.

Chapter Twenty-Six

All the Friends were surrounding the cemetery in a circle. New, Mid, and Old, in all their different iterations. *My* Friends, the ones I had known in this life, were standing together at a solitary headstone in the middle of the cemetery. The only one that hadn't been consumed by the rot.

"Hello there," I said to my three Friends.

They curtsied in response.

Holding the baby, I walked to them. It was difficult. My body was covered in rot, my bones brittle, my joints creaking and cracking like an old wooden rocking chair. I remembered the days I more resembled New Friend than Old and longed for that youth once more.

There was a ruckus in the sky. I looked up. Mom and Dad were there, entwined, him thrusting into her amongst the stars.

Time was fluid. Everything and nothing was here at once, in this place, and I had to choose.

Not meant to be.
Save everyone.
Save her.

Lavo had never meant to destroy everything. Everything was already destroyed. Aamon hadn't wanted destroyed. He wanted everything to *remain* destroyed.

I placed the baby on the grave. As soon as she was out of my arms, I turned to my Friends. They were all the parts of me; light and dark, but a mismatched jumble, like a version of me I didn't know how to assemble. I held out my arms and we embraced. I felt a tickle on my legs, a wisp of pleasure on my sex as Gus scurried up inside of me, back home one last time.

"Do it," I said to my Friends.

They knew just what to do because they were me. New Friend drove her nails into my sternum, splitting my skin with scalpel-like precision. Friend used her powerful, arachnid arms to grasp my ribs and crack them open, exposing the organs beneath. Old Friend looked into my eyes, her milky vision clouding with tears.

"We've lived a life, haven't we, Old Friend," I said, blood trickling from the corners of my mouth.

She smiled, revealing a toothless maw and grey tongue. I hesitated, so she hesitated, but New Friend and Friend put a hand on each of her shoulders, encouraging her.

Old Friend kissed my cheek, then tenderly wrapped her arthritic fingers around the three hearts in my chest cavity. My mom's heart, my dad's heart, and mine.

I looked up into the trees, at Trebor, my dad. Old Friend peeled his heart away from the other two and bit into it, black blood squirting out and marring her grey face. Dad's heart had been sour long before I'd put it in a jar after I killed him, long before I consumed it in the backyard of my house in Eden's Edge. As Old Friend bit off another chunk and swallowed, Trebor turned to static, his image glitching in and out each time I blinked. In the distance, Aamon screeched, and plumes of flame flickered over the woods. Old Friend swallowed the last bite with an audible gulp and Trebor was gone, Aamon's screeches silenced, the flame extinguished.

Next was Mom's heart. Old Friend ate it slow, and I tasted it along with her; the flavour in my mouth was sweet and savoury—fresh bread and honey. Mom stood beside me and spoke, though her words carried no sound. I read on her lips the words that had carried me through time.

You are smart. You are strong.

I love you.

Then Mom was gone.

The last heart was all mine. Neither witch nor demon, but a melding of me and all three friends. Old Friend held it out, and New Friend and Friend held the heart with her. Together, they lowered the heart down to the baby and placed it in her chest. Like writhing tree roots, the arteries and capillaries began to connect, braiding together, and my world went dark.

Chapter Twenty-Seven

"See?" Laz said to Mary. "No ghosts."

What was happening? Where was I?

With a hand on her hip and a roll of her eyes, Mary said, "Duh, you idiot. It's daytime. They're allergic to the sun."

"They ain't vampires," Laz said. "That's not how it works."

"If it ain't real, then how does it work at all then?" Mary said, head tilted so her curls draped on her shoulder.

"Stop." Liza said. "Show some respect."

"The dead don't care," Laz said.

Mary opened her mouth, an argument on her tongue, but Liza held up a hand. "I meant respect each other."

I was back in the cemetery, all those years ago, before my friends were ruined and everything went to shit. We were all children once again.

I was laid out like New Friend had been, in front of a headstone like Sleeping Beauty on her funeral slab, and blood oozed out of my open chest cavity.

I spoke, my voice so very far away. "I can see." Plump, juicy leaves shuddered in the breath of a gentle breeze. I saw the trees, some dead and rotting, some solid and healthy. All the wood, dead or alive, was teeming with life—insects, incisor marks from deer and rabbits, hidey holes that rodents used as homes and playgrounds. I saw the emerald shimmer of the grass and the roan dirt of the forest floor.

"I can hear." Birdsong trilled in my ears, twittering and warbling in time with the rustling of the leaves. In the distance, there was water, but it was far, bubbling and gurgling and streaming over boulders, lapping against shores of mud and roots.

"I can smell." Forest. Pine. Critters. Flowers. Wood fires burning in the distance.

"I can taste." No salt water—the ocean must have been far—but I could taste the mustiness in the air from mold and dust. And there was the lack of taste as well. No smoke, no petrol, no stench of concrete jungle.

"I can feel ..." breeze caressing my skin, the tickle of grave grass poking through my tights, the soft petals of a wild rose as I pinched it. I rolled the petals until they smeared between the pressure of my fingertips, and I thought of flesh— of me pulling and tearing, pinching a vein until it burst like a balloon. The wet of the annihilated wild rose became crimson gore rather than smeared fuchsia on the milky hue of my skin.

"Huh," Liza said. "Nature nut, eh?"

I was no longer nervous. Nature had calmed me, like it had done my whole life. I gazed at Liza, right into her dark eyes. *How beautiful*, I thought, *should stars glitter there in the black.*

"Are you okay, Anna?" Liza asked.

"I feel fine," I said.

When I was little, it had been New Friend on this grave, struggling against unseen bindings. Red marks appeared on her wrists as she rotated them back and forth, her fingers clawing the dirt for purchase. Her feet flexed and her ankle bones knocked together as she tried to free her legs from something that grasped her that I could not see. Was she screaming? Maybe. Her stomach was heaving, her shoulders lifting off the ground as her core twisted and turned. An imaginary weight was upon her, pinning her down.

But there was no weight on me now. Nothing holding me back. I had knowledge now that I didn't have then, power I hadn't realized.

I rolled to my hands and knees and crawled away as the sounds of Mary and Laz's play faded to a muffled droning. Liza was saying something, but her voice, too, was far away and encased in maple syrup.

"I'll be back," I said, and I walked into the woods.

I walked and Old Man Merle followed, warding off anything that might stop me.

I arrived in Eden's Edge, as it was back then. All buildings intact, the Beast looming above all else.

I ascended the stairs to Miss Mojo and gave her a hug. She was alive again, all human, radiating love and joy... Her brow furrowed in confusion before her face went slack, and her mouth curved into a sad smile.

"I love you, child," she said. "You do your thing, now."

I wondered if she knew what she could have become. A swarm of bees, a kaleidoscope of butterflies. She might know one day, but not until she'd had a chance to live her full life.

"Goodbye," I said.

She laughed and cried, a jolly sound, and we embraced one last time before I left the Beast, en route for the fated house perched at the edge of Eden like a predator.

Chapter Twenty-Eight

I rapped on the wood of Allison's door; each knock a threat.

The door opened.

"What do you want?" she snapped. "You should be at school."

I stepped inside, shoving a shoulder into Allison as I entered her den.

She followed me, fingers fumbling at the buttons on her blouse as she finished dressing herself.

"Did I interrupt?" I asked, motioning to her clothing.

"Pardon?" she asked.

Her lipstick was slightly smeared off her thin lips, her skirt rumpled.

"I can smell Bobby's rotten cock on you, but no seed," I said. "Not yet. He's going to be mad if you don't finish him off."

Her mouth dropped open, her brows scrunched in fury.

"And if Bobby doesn't finish on you, or in you, he's

likely to go after my friends and finish in them," I said. I did not hold back my tears of rage as I spoke, but the calm that enveloped me was heavy, feigning the appearance of calm...

"You little … you … you cannot speak to me like that!" Allison shrieked. "You are a child!"

"Not anymore," I said.

There was no need for anything grand or performative. My talons shot out, and I effortlessly sliced my arm through the air, severing Allison's head in one swipe. It dropped to the floor with a muted thud, her body crumpling next to it shortly after. As her blood spurted into a pool that soaked into her designer rug, the door to the basement opened and Bobby emerged, tucking his now flaccid dick into his stained jeans.

"The fuck?" he said.

I lined up and kicked Allison's head at him, nailing him directly in the face. He screamed and stumbled backward, failing to catch himself and tumbling down the stairs, head over heels. I retracted my talons as I descended the stairs, beholding his broken body laid out on the concrete floor.

Bobby was screaming something resembling words, but I didn't care. I just needed him to stay conscious, keep screaming.

"You will never be inside another human," I said as I reached the bottom of the stair. "You will never feel another ounce of power or pleasure. And every bit of those things you have felt in your miserable life, I will erase for you with the memory of this."

His bladder released and tears poured from his eyes. He pleaded, sputtered, sniveled. His neck was broken, his arms and legs dead appendages that could not fight me off. I unzipped his jeans and shimmied them off, then sliced his shirt off. He wailed as I hoisted him up on the wall and suspended him where he would have suspended Laz.

I ruined him there on that wall, like he ruined so many people, until his body was in shreds and his heart gave in.

But his screams never stopped. And as he hung there, for all of eternity, they never would.

Chapter Twenty-Nine

When I walked back through Eden's Edge, it was crackling. There was no fire to see or feel, but it was there. Back in the future where I had left Aamon vomiting flame.

He was trying to kill Lavo's beetles who were cleaning everything, leaving it shiny new. Cleansing the future that could have been.

The walk was longer than ever. Day burned into the ash of night as I traversed the forest path. Around me, things from beyond the veil were tearing the earth, downing trees, chewing up flora and fauna. Nature was fighting back, sharp sticks puncturing eyeballs of snarling things that frothed at the mouth, animals tearing at feathered or leathered flesh. I realized I was on neither side of the veil, but somewhere in between, watching both sides destruct.

When I crossed the threshold into the cemetery, the scene was familiar, almost identical, though it was no longer daytime. It was full night, the moon alighting the world. Laz and Mary were playing, warring with sticks and stones as they had been. Liza was laid out on the grass, propped on her elbows, gazing at the stars above.

They didn't see me, between the veil as I was.

"Where did the new kid go?" Laz asked.

Liza's brow furled. She searched the cemetery as if a fog had lifted.

"Back home, I guess," Mary said with a shrug.

The grave where New Friend had been laying, where *I* had been laying, was open, dirt piled high to the side. And standing around it was a mourning circle—Mom, Miss Mojo in the flesh, Marie, Old Man Merle. Claw-like hands attached to pale arms reached from the open grave, grasping, feeling for me. I walked to the edge of the expanse and peered in.

New Friend, Friend, and Old Friend were inside. Old Friend had the baby in her arms, rocking it, the infant's lips sealed around her engorged nipple.

Erinyes landed on my mom's shoulder. Mom was crying but her face was smiling.

"You are smart," she said. "You are strong."

"I love you," I said . . .

I hugged my mom and breathed in her scent. It would linger in my mind forever.

Miss Mojo was sobbing fat, juicy tears, a smile on her ruby lips. I smooshed into her, suffocating myself in the mass of her breasts.

"Child," she said, and she kissed my lips.

"Love ye," I said.

Marie and I gave each other a knowing look. A long, solid embrace.

I waved to the forest, to Kaz and Kendra, who stood hand-in-hand.

I looked to the edge of the grave. Old Man Merle was there. He wouldn't look at me. His face was snarled into a pout.

"Merle," I said, touching his arm.

"GAHHHH!" he bellowed.

"I have to," I said. "But this isn't the end."

I hugged him, and eventually, he hugged back. The movement of his sobs finally drew my tears, and we cried into each other, holding each other as the baby below began to coo.

New Friend, Friend, and Old Friend were holding up the baby, six hands supporting her, raising her out of the grave. I released Old Man Merle, and he took the bundle, his face joyous as he cradled the baby in his arms.

I stepped close to the grave, so close that my toes curled over the edge. The six hands grabbed me and pulled me into the hole. The four of us fused together, one at last. At the mouth of the grave above, the bundle in Merle's arms squalled and contorted, skin stretching, tearing, squealing as bones cracked, separated, elongated until the baby was a child, standing on her own, her hand in Merle's.

The last time I saw her, I was dead. I was in a grave, looking up at the sky, stars like speckled paint across the never-ending indigo. There was an earthworm crawling through my sinuses. I realized, after noticing it slithering through my facial cavities, that my mouth was full of wet dirt. Packed full, puffing my cheeks out like a squirrel's. Then the stars disappeared, eclipsed by a looming shape.

Her face and body were dark, a silhouette against the night sky, but her eyes were glowing. One blue, one dark hazel, twinkling with stars of their own. Her hair was an explosion of curls, dark and light, and in her chest beat a single heart, pure and true. My heart and mine alone.

The sky above me burst with colour—dancing greens and blues that shone in the baby's eyes.

"Aurora," I said. Goddess of dawn, the beauty and vitality of a new day.

"Mom," she said, tears rolling down her freckled

cheeks, her voice a perfect melody.
   A piece of me, a part of Liza. Pure joy and beauty.
   My heart, my love, my second chance.

Chapter Thirty
EPILOGUE

The first time I saw her, she was dead. She was both my mom and me, my maker and her death. She was so beautiful, lying there, embraced by all versions of herself: New Friend, Friend, and Old Friend. They looked so peaceful, minds finally at rest.

I would do her proud. Make the most of this second shot at life.

"What are you lookin' at, Aurora?" Laz called from the trees.

I blinked, and the hole was filled. Overgrown with grass as though there'd never been a hole there at all. I glanced over at the lychgate. Perfectly intact, straight, no gateway there at all. The rot was gone, had never been there, not in this version.

"Nothin'," I said as I pushed at the grass with the toe of my black patent shoe.

She was under there, my mom, my maker. I vowed I

would visit her, tell her about my life, about all the things that I would do that she never could.

A small patch of grass heaved, and a tiny paw emerged. Then a second paw, and a sniffling snout. I dropped to my knees and plunged my hands into the dirt, scooping it aside, trying to not make too big a mess.

"Awww!" Mary said as she came skipping over. "A baby!"

I pulled a little squirrel from the dirt. He should have been dead, but he wasn't. He should have suffocated, but I knew he didn't need air. I knew he'd live forever, with me. He was plump, fluffy, and full of naughtiness, just like me. Just like Mom would have been, had she had the chance.

"Hello Gus," I said.

Gus climbed up the straps of my pinafore, came to rest on my shoulder, and nuzzled into my neck.

"They'll never let you keep him," Liza said. "Miss Mojo doesn't allow animals in the foster home."

Oh right. I had no mom, not one that lived above the worms and dirt. That's okay. Miss Mojo was amazing. And there were no predators in Eden's Edge to worry about. Not anymore.

"I suspect she'll make an exception for Gus," I said.

Laz and Mary exchanged puzzled looks, then shrugged it off and continued to play amongst the headstones.

Liza watched me carefully.

I touched my hair, the black and ice-blonde curls spro-inging though my fingers. Liza puzzled over me, searching my face. My mind was static, knowing but forgetting. Starting from scratch with a lifetime of knowledge that was pleas-antly out of reach.

"You have two different coloured eyes," Liza said. "How come? I didn't notice until now …"

Because I wasn't born until just now.

"Uh huh," I said. "Got them from my mom."

I placed my hand on my chest and felt the single heart within the cage of my ribs, beating steady and strong.

"Whatever happened to your parents?" Liza asked.

"My mom died in childbirth," I said. "She was beautiful, hair like a raven's feathers, eyes like pools of black gold."

"And your dad?" Liza asked.

I didn't know how to tell her. To explain it, to explain *me*.

"My other mom gave her life to make me," I said. "To make a second chance for me, and for herself. For everyone."

Liza cocked a brow, her lips parting to say something.

Those lips were so beautiful. I bet they tasted sweet and felt like silk.

"You're weird," Liza said.

"Yeah," I said. "I'm me."

I didn't give Liza a chance to respond. I ran to her, grabbing her hand from the grass and pulling her to her feet. We chased each other around the cemetery, laughing as we dodged butterflies and flowers until all four of us were yawning and we made out way back to Eden's Edge.

We would grow, we would laugh, we would learn through Miss Mojo's tutelage. Eden's Edge would be home until we ventured out in adulthood, tasting youth, college, relationships, jobs, families, life.

I would always return to Eden's Edge, to the cottage I called home, and I would sit in the chair made by the man in the single yellow boot. I would close my eyes and feel the smiles upon me, people from a distant life I could no longer remember well. Red wings would flap on my chest, butterflies would flutter on my cheeks, and there was a sound in the distance, a familiar voice.

Gahhhh.

"I love you."

I said it to Mom, to Old Man Merle, to Gus and Erinyes, to Marie and Miss Mojo. To Liza, who waited for me in our home, with our children.

Thanks to them, I am smart, I am strong.
I am happy.

THE END

* * *

About the Author

Jae Mazer is a Canadian who was born in Victoria, British Columbia, and grew up in the prairies of Northern Alberta. After spending the majority of her life battling sasquatches in the Great White North, she migrated south to Texas to have a go at the armadillos. She is a connoisseur and creator of gothic horror, splatterfolk, splatter westerns, and folk horror. She's degreed, won awards, been in anthologies, has chameleon hair and lots of skin ink, and enjoys mustard and alcohol.

Awards:

- ATAI 2017, WINNER, Best Horror Novel for *Chrysalis and Clan*
- American Book Fest 2019, Best Horror Novel for *Crone: A Witch's Tale*

- Next Generation Indie Book Awards 2019 Runner-up/Finalist for *Crone: A Witch's Tale*
- Next Generation Indie Book Awards 2021 Runner-up/Finalist for *Blood Wail*.
- New York City Midnight Finalist for Short Screenplay for *Just Like Momma*

OTHER HELLBOUND BOOKS

The First Time I Saw Her

Anna and her mother are on the run after a tragedy shatters their world. A stranger has offered them protection in a private community hidden deep in the woods, and Anna and her mother have no choice but to abandon their life and belongings to take refuge until they can figure out their next move.

But the woman who helped them may not be what she seems, and the safe-haven community has its own secrets ... and its own dangers.

Anna is no ordinary girl, though. She can perceive things others cannot, impossible things. Now thrust into an unfamiliar setting with horrors unfolding all around her, Anna must figure out what she is and what she is capable of before she loses what little she has left of her life.

THE FIRST TIME I SAW HER is the first installment in the Gossamer and Pitch Trilogy, a series about love and hate, witches and demons, and the sheer veil between life and death.

The Next Time I Saw Her

After the catastrophe at Eden's Edge, Anna finds herself living on the streets, hiding from the foster care system and her own identity. She survives her way into adulthood, and now lives in an apartment in the city, holding down a job as a bartender and flying under the radar.

But Anna's past has come to find her. Inexplicable murders occur within Anna's vicinity, and she can't help but notice the links to her childhood. Joined by some of her old friends, and a few new ones, Anna fights to prove her innocence while being forced to face the truth of what she really is.

THE NEXT TIME I SAW HER is book two in the Gossamer and Pitch Trilogy. It is a splatterfolk tale full of blood, demons, sexuality, body horror, and trauma. Join Anna as she navigates this season of her life.

Satan Rides Your Daughter Again

Welcome to the second volume of HellBound's satanic-themed anthology, our homage to all things Old Nick and those who worship him and his demonic underlings!

From a poor woman suffering at the hands of witch finders, the building of an infamous Bunny Ranch and absolute living Hell that is high school, to encounters with angels, Hades' pit, the quest for a hellishly good chilli, and so much more in between, Satan Rides Your Daughter Again is packed with devilishly good tales to torment your soul with a taste of the fire and brimstone underworld that roils below us…

Featuring some of the very best independent horror authors committing words to paper today: R.D. Tyler, Dan Bolden, K A Douglas, Dylan Bosworth, Conor O'Brian Barnes, Dan Muenzer, Josh Darling, Barend Nieuwstraten III, Matthew Fryer, Kevin L. Kennel, J Louis Messina, Terry Grimwood, James Musgrave, Donn L. Hess, Shannon Lawrence, Chase Hughes, KT Bartlett, Sarah Goodman, Mariah Southworth, and Terry Campbell.

HellBound Highway

We invite you, fellow horror aficionados, to take a ride on HellBound Highway – a terrifying trip into the darkest recesses of the human mind you'd care to discover, your ticket to ride provided by a bunch of the very best authors writing on the independent horror scene today.

Of course, it's not your ordinary ticket, it's a boarding pass to twenty-eight sinister tales about terror excursions you most definitely wouldn't want to experience first-hand.

Two Headed Alligator

Despite being conjoined twins with one heart between them, Deirdre and Desdemona Gardner lived perfectly ordinary lives until they turned fourteen, when strange clicking noises in the night and a string of missing girls turned their quiet existence into a waking nightmare.

In the wake of an unspeakable tragedy, the twins spent a summer away from home, visiting a small Louisiana town with a dark history of murder, unsolved disappearances, and lynching – all centered around two figures fascinating to Deirdre: Florence and Sage Labelle, conjoined twins, alligator farm heiresses, and suspected serial killers.

With the help of Florence's diary and a mysterious little girl whose uncannily adult mannerisms, antiquated vocabulary, and extensive knowledge of her town's history set Desdemona on edge, the Gardner twins set out to solve a decades-old murder mystery while struggling to cope with their own traumatic past.

Following a semi-successful separation surgery, the surviving twin, wishing to remain anonymous, invites you to read this, her life story.

A HellBound Books LLC
Publication

www.hellboundbooks.com

SIGN UP FOR THE HELLBOUND BOOKS NEWSLETTER:

Printed in the United States of America

9 781966 296232